LAVENDER AND A MESSY BLUNDER

A FERN GROVE COZY MYSTERY

ABBY REEDE

PEN-N-A-PAD PUBLISHING

OTHER BOOKS IN THE FERN GROVE SERIES

Carnations and Deadly Fixations

One Daisy and Two Crazy Funerals

White Lily and a Fatal Chili

Mistletoe and Deadly Kisses

Freesia and Lethal Amnesia

Daffodils and Poisonous Pills

A FERN GROVE COZY MYSTERY

BOOK TEN

Tracy felt her eyes were glazing over. Her back was stiff, her neck ached, and she was ready to stand up and stretch her arms over her head. She had been sitting at Grind it Out, the local coffee shop, for nearly two hours as her friend, Isabella, lamented over her unsuccessful job hunt. While Tracy credited herself with being a good friend and a wonderful listener, as the minutes ticked by, she wished she could just end the conversation.

"I'm just over-qualified," Isabella complained as Tracy snapped back to attention. "I have a business degree from Syracuse and a certificate in technology from Brown, and no one will hire me. What kind of place is this?"

"A small town," Tracy interjected. "You have to adjust your expectations, Isabella. This isn't Seattle, LA, or New York. This is like the minor, minor leagues."

Isabella scrunched up her nose. "I can't even rely on my old backup plan here," she frowned. "It's not like anyone needs *models* in this town."

Tracy exhaled slowly. Isabella was beautiful *and* brilliant, but she was driving Tracy crazy with her endless complaining. Tracy knew her friend was still adjusting to her new life in Tracy's tiny hometown, but after three weeks of hearing about Isabella's antics as she searched for work, Tracy half wished her best friend had just stayed in Portland where the two had first met.

"Hey?"

Isabella's voice caught Tracy's attention. "What? Sorry."

Her friend raised an eyebrow. "You aren't even listening to me."

"I am," Tracy insisted. "Sorry, I'm so tired. I didn't sleep well last night."

Her friend studied her face. "What, pre-wedding jitters already?"

Tracy's wedding to Warren, a local detective, was coming up in a few months. Most of the planning was finished, but every now and then, Tracy could not sleep as visions of tablescapes, passed hors d'oeuvres, and plates of salmon, chicken, and beef danced through her head.

"No, I just had a bad dream."

Isabella nodded sympathetically, but then returned to her diatribe about the job market in the small town. "It's like everyone is out to get me, you know? Why won't someone hire the big city girl with the shiny resume? It's a joke, Tracy. A total joke…"

Just then, Tracy's phone began to ring. She held up a finger to silence her friend. "Sorry," she mouthed as she answered the call. "It's Warren."

"Babe," her fiancé's deep voice greeted her cheerfully. "How are you doing?"

"I'm fine, honey," she answered, though she was ready to run out of the coffee shop and leave her friend behind. "What's up?"

"Great news," he shared. "You know the big case I have been working on?"

"The missing woman from Kingsbury?"

"Yes!"

Tracy gripped the phone tightly. "What's the news?"

"She has been found!"

Tracy's heart fluttered. "That's great news!"

"She's alive and well, and that means I am leaving the office early tonight for the first time in a month. How do you feel about a little dinner out together to celebrate?"

She grinned. Warren had been putting in extra hours for the last few weeks, and she was elated at the prospect of a date night.

"Absolutely," she agreed. "Where should we go?"

"I'll take you somewhere nice," he told her. "Why don't you wear that pretty purple dress? The one you wore for our anniversary date?"

She felt herself blush as she remembered their extravagant date to Portland, seeing a musical and dining at a French restaurant. It had been one of the best nights of her life.

"What time will you be home?" she asked.

"I'll pick you up at six-thirty," he replied.

Tracy glanced down at her watch. It was only noon, but this gave her the perfect excuse to leave her coffee date with Isabella. "That's so soon," she said, feigning concern. "I'll have to leave now and start getting ready."

"Soon? You have all day," he laughed, but she was not going to blow her cover.

"I will be in such a rush," she fretted, rising to her feet. "I have to say goodbye to Isabella and hurry out of the coffee shop to get home. See you soon, honey!"

She hung up the phone and shrugged apologetically at Isabella. "He's taking me on a special date soon," she fibbed. "I have to go home and get ready. Sorry to cut our coffee date short!"

Isabella groaned. "Back to the grind for me, I guess."

Tracy reached over to hug her friend before dashing out the door. "Hang in there!"

That evening, dressed in her purple halter neck dress and a pair of matching high heels, her hair piled atop her head in an elegant chignon, Tracy waited eagerly for her fiance to pick her up from her apartment. She had spent nearly an hour doing her makeup, and she could hardly wait to see Warren's face when he saw her.

She heard a knock at the door, and her heart beat excitedly as she raced to open it. Standing before her was her tall, handsome fiance. He was wearing a mint green button-up shirt with a satin tie, matching socks, and a pair of mocha-colored dress shoes. She rarely saw him outside of his uniform or casual clothing, and Tracy could even detect the rich scent of his best cologne.

"Honey, you look amazing," she exclaimed as she ran into his arms. "And your cologne! You really dressed up for me."

His eyes were fixed on her. "No, look at *you*," he countered as he gazed lovingly at her. "My almost wife is a beauty. That dress was *made* for you."

She spun around, giving the tulle skirt a twirl. The dress *was* her favorite piece of clothing. Before moving back to her hometown, she had lived in Portland and worked in a prestigious finance job at a bank. She always had a rotation of company cocktail parties, happy hours, and events on her calendar, and she had bought this purple dress for her office's annual holiday party. The A-line shape and halter neck highlighted her womanly figure, drawing attention to her curves and making her waist look small.

"Maybe I should get rid of my wedding dress and just wear this," she suggested playfully.

"I wouldn't mind," he winked. He held out his hand and took hers, giving it a squeeze. "Come on, let's go. We have a reservation at La Vida."

"La Vida?" she cried with joy. "I've always wanted to go there."

"I know," he grinned. "You have been such a good sport while I have been so busy with work, so tonight, we'll celebrate the end of this case at La Vida."

When they arrived at the restaurant, Tracy was instantly impressed with the modern decor, the low lighting, and the immaculately styled waitstaff. They were greeted by a tall, lithe woman in a black dress, and she led them to their table, a two-top next to the window. Warren politely pulled out the buttery leather chair for Tracy, and she sank into the seat with a smile on her face.

The hostess poured them water from a glass vase on the table and nodded. "Rafa will be right with you. He will be taking care of you tonight."

"Thanks," Tracy told her, cringing as she heard her voice squeak as the hostess walked away.

"Babe, are you sure we can afford this? This restaurant looks like a museum, and I think a meal here might cost as much as a month of my rent."

He held a finger to his lips and pretended to quiet her. "Babe, stop. It's my treat. You've been a trooper, and I want to celebrate the end of this case. The outcome was more than we could hope for, and it's worth celebrating."

He held up his water glass and took a sip. "Yum, it's sparkling!"

They ordered appetizers and cocktails, admiring the taste and presentation of each item. When it was finally time to place their dinner order, Tracy decided on a tuna steak while Warren selected the duck breast.

"I hope the portions are large so I can take my tuna home for lunch tomorrow," she commented as their server walked away. "But I know fancy restaurants don't give you that much."

"Just enjoy tonight," he urged her. "Don't think about tomorrow."

The familiar strains of the song "Don't Stop Believing" by Journey began to play, and Tracy looked at her fiance. "Is that your cell phone?"

He pulled it out of his pocket and read the screen. "Sorry, I should have turned it off," he apologized as he silenced the incoming call. Ten seconds later, the phone rang again.

"Sorry," he told her as he shook his head. "I need to turn the sound off..."

She cocked her head to the side. "Who is calling you?" she asked.

Warren turned down the volume, but the phone began to ring again. "Ugh..."

"Warren? Who is it?"

His eyes widened as he shoved the phone into his pocket. "No one. It's nothing."

Tracy furrowed her bow. "What's going on?" she asked. "You're acting weird. Who was calling you?"

He crossed his arms over his chest. "Does it matter?"

She felt her stomach churn. "I'm your fiance," she declared. "The most important person in your life. Why are you being so weird and awkward about who was calling you?"

He took a deep breath. "I don't think you want to know."

Tracy felt her heart begin to race. "What are you talking about? Warren, what is going on?"

He looked down at the table and closed his eyes. "The phone call..." he began. "It was Charlie."

2

Tracy blinked. She did not know what she had been expecting, but her fiance receiving a call from Charlie, his best friend of fifteen years, was not out of the ordinary.

"Ok? What's so wild about Charlie calling you that you would act so weird?"

He bit his lip. "Charlie is organizing my bachelor party," he said softly. "I wasn't sure how you felt about bachelor parties, and I didn't want you to find out this way…"

Tracy raised an eyebrow. "Why do you think I am opposed to you having a bachelor party?" she questioned. "I've never held you back from having fun with your friends, have I?"

"No!" he insisted. "I guess I just assumed you wouldn't be excited for me because you are not having a bachelorette party."

She frowned. "They are stupid," she announced. "Making your friends pay hundreds or thousands of dollars to celebrate your decision to legalize your relationship feels pretty selfish."

"Ouch," he cringed. "Is that all you think our marriage will be? Legalizing our relationship?"

She saw the hurt in his eyes. "No!" she insisted. "I'm sorry. I didn't mean for it to come out that way. Our marriage is so important to me, and it means so much, Warren. I promise."

He stared at her. "Then what is your problem with bachelor or bachelorette parties?"

Tracy huffed. "My cousin, Kyla, insisted on the most extravagant bachelorette party. We had to fly to Cabo, pay thousands of dollars for a resort, buy her lingerie, *and* pay for her share in everything. It was ridiculous. I was in college then and had to eat ramen for a month straight to afford it all."

Warren studied her face. "That really ruined it for you, huh?"

"Well, yeah," she told him. "It just felt so self-indulgent, and Kyla got divorced six months after the wedding, anyway!"

Warren sighed. "I was worried you would be like this," he murmured.

"What? These are valid points," she argued. "Weddings are expensive, and our friends will already have to fly in and get hotel rooms for our wedding weekend. Why make them do more?"

"To make memories," he told her. "To spend time together. To celebrate the end of an era and a new chapter."

She sat up in her seat. "Those are nice sentiments," she agreed. "But what if something happens?"

"If something happens? Like if I died or got hurt?"

"Worse." Tracy's eyes grew large with concern. "My college roommate's younger sister, Kimmy, was supposed to get married a few years ago. At the bachelor party in Tulum, her fiance cheated on her with a local girl. The local girl messaged Kimmy from the fiance's phone and the wedding got called off."

Warren's face crumbled. "You think I could do that to you?"

Tracy realized she had crossed a line. "No, no!" she insisted. "I'm sorry, that was uncalled for."

"It really was," Warren agreed. "I love you, Tracy, and I would never compromise our relationship."

"I know," she chimed in. "I am so sorry, babe. I've just heard horror stories about parties like that, and it's really impacted my perspective. I know you would never do anything to lose me. I'm sure your party will be fun. It's not like Charlie is planning some wild weekend in Vegas or something!"

She saw the color drain from her fiance's face. "Oh," she said softly. "So… you are going to Las Vegas?"

"Just for a few nights," he promised. "And most of the guys on the trip are married or in serious relationships. Some even have children! It will be relaxing and fun and nothing like any of the horror stories you've heard."

Tracy felt a knot in her stomach. She wanted to seem secure and collected, but she hated the idea of her future husband even being in Las Vegas, let alone going to day clubs or casinos.

"I love you," he continued, reaching across the table and taking her hand. "I promise that you have nothing to worry about."

She took a deep breath and forced herself to smile. "Okay," she agreed. "You're right. I have nothing to worry about."

When she got home from her date, she frantically called Isabella. When her friend didn't answer, she texted her: **911. Call me.**

Isabella called her back instantly. "What's up?"

"Did you screen my call?" Tracy chided her.

"I'm watching an Oprah rerun," Isabella sniffed. "It's part of my self-care routine."

"Sorry to interrupt then," Tracy said.

"What's up? 911?" Isabella inquired. "Aren't you supposed to be on a hot date or something?"

Tracy cleared her throat. "I was on my date," she shared. "And then Warren dropped a bomb on me…"

"What is it?" Isabella asked, her interest clearly piqued. "Does he have a secret love child? Is he a foreign spy? Is he being called up by the FBI and you two are moving to Saudi Arabia for a secret mission?"

Tracy laughed in spite of herself. "What? Where did you come up with those ideas? Oprah?"

"It's a very interesting Oprah episode," Isabella told her. "A lot is happening."

"Clearly."

"What did he say?" Isabella demanded. "What's the big 911 news?"

Tracy took a deep breath, not wanting to sound childish or petty. "He's having a bachelor party in Las Vegas."

"Okay?"

"Las Vegas," she repeated, enunciating every vowel. "For his bachelor party."

"So what? At least he isn't going to Atlantic City or Mykonos or Barcelona. I hear that's where the real fun is to be had."

Tracy felt like her friend was not understanding her predicament. "Isabella, I just feel weird about him going off for this wild party when I am not having a bachelorette party."

"Let's fix that, then," Isabella suggested breezily. "Let's throw you a bachelorette party. It's decided."

"What?" Tracy exclaimed. "Me? A bachelorette party?"

She heard Isabella snapping her gum. "Why not? You are getting married, and a bachelorette party is a tradition."

"Don't you think it's too cliche or self-indulgent?" Tracy worried. "What will people think?"

"That you are a bride in her thirties who is ready to make lifelong memories with her best friends before she says I do? Come on, Tracy. Don't be a square. I will plan the trip of a lifetime, and you won't be sorry about it."

"Really?" she asked hopefully. "You think it will be fun?"

Isabella laughed. "Have we met? Do you think I am capable of planning a bad party? Remember the Friendsgiving celebration I hosted a few years ago in Portland? Or the

Hanukkah party? Or the Easter brunch? I am the planning queen, Tracy. Trust me."

"Okay," she agreed, nodding her head. "So… I am having a bachelorette party! It's official!"

"Yes, it is," Isabella confirmed. "And I promise you it will be a trip to *die* for!"

3

Three days later, Tracy was hard at work at In Season, the flower shop that her Aunt Rose owned and operated. Tracy had started working there when she moved back to town, and she enjoyed meeting customers and the simplicity of the work she did for them. Along with Tracy's aunt, Tiffany, a young local woman, also worked at the shop, and the trio created incredible flower arrangements for all occasions.

As Tracy clipped the thorns off of a yellow rose, the front door opened and Isabella strutted in. She was dressed stylishly in a pair of tight red leather pants, a beige sleeveless tunic top, and a pair of wedge sandals. From her attire, it was clear she was not a local, and Tracy wondered if her friend would ever adjust her wardrobe to match the low-key, casual nature of the town.

"It's done," Isabella declared as she swooped in. "The party planning is done."

"Party?" Tiffany asked as she emerged from the back room. "Tracy's bachelorette party?"

Isabella nodded. "Yes! The reservations are made and everything is ready for our trip next week. I have the decorations ready, the gift bags assembled, and wait until you see the location. It is *so* Tracy!" Isabella gushed.

Tracy had not seen her friend this excited in a long time. "Where are we going?" she asked. "Charleston? La Jolla? The Keys?"

Isabella shrugged playfully. "I can't tell! Trust me, though. You will love it, Tracy. We'll have the best time."

Aunt Rose bustled out of the office. "Did you settle on a location, Isabella?"

"I did! But I can't give it away. I want it to be a surprise for Tracy," she beamed.

"Oh, that will be so sweet. Well, can I help you with anything?" Rose offered. "I can help with some of the planning or organize some of the meals?"

Isabella shook her head. "No, no, and no! I have it all taken care of."

Tiffany smiled. "Are you sure? I can help, too! I know a party shop with a lot of cool decorations. I could stop by after work and stock up."

"NO." Isabella replied firmly. "I know what I am doing. At the last dinner party I hosted, the wife of one of my friends, who is a professional chef, said that I should go into event planning. She was so impressed with my menu and the ambience. Trust me, I've got this."

"Okay, okay," Rose backed off. "Well, Tracy, do you need any help getting ready? Is there anything you need to get ready for the trip?"

Tracy nodded. "I am not sure how to pack," she admitted. "If we are going to the beach, I need a few things. If we are going to a city, I might need to get a new pair of heels. I'm just not sure. Isabella, are you sure you can't give me a hint?"

"No way," her friend told her. "No hints. And pack it *all*!"

* * *

Tracy plucked nervously at the blindfold wound tightly around her head. She could not see anything, and she felt like Isabella was hitting every pothole along Interstate 5.

"Are we almost there?" she asked, thinking they were en route to the airport. "I'm feeling a little carsick…"

"Do you want some water?" Tiffany offered. "I have some in my purse."

"That's okay," she shook her head. "I don't like to hydrate before I fly. It makes it harder to fall asleep on the plane when I have to go to the bathroom every ten minutes."

She heard her aunt giggle. "What? Why are you laughing?"

"Oh, nothing," Rose promised, but Tracy heard the glee in her voice.

"Two minutes away!" Isabella divulged as the van she had rented took a sharp right turn. "We are pulling up right now."

Tracy anxiously pawed at the blindfold. "Come on, tell me where we are going," she pleaded. "Should I be mentally prepared for a long flight or a short one? Two hours? Six hours? A long haul?"

"It's a surprise!" Isabella sang. "Wait one more minute and you will find out."

Tracy felt the car come to an abrupt stop. "Are we here? Do we need to hop out? Are you able to park on the curb so we can unload our bags? I need to make a quick bathroom trip before we hit the security line."

Isabella turned off the car. "Okay, this looks a bit different," Tracy heard her mutter.

"Is this what it looked like online?" Rose whispered back.

"No, but I think it'll be fine," Isabella replied.

Tracy reached her hands up and tore the blindfold from her temples. "Okay, I need to know what's going on," she declared. "Where are we?"

She blinked as the brightness of the morning sun flooded her vision. She looked out the window and was shocked to not be parked at the airport.

"Where are we?" she asked, glancing around at the green, rolling landscape. "Are we in the country?"

"Wine country!" Isabella squealed. "Welcome to Greenhithe Falls, the wine capital of the Pacific Northwest!"

Tracy peered outside and saw endless fields, ramshackle barns, and a small blue A-frame house with a man standing outside of it. "Are we here?"

"This is it," Rose confirmed. "Welcome to your special weekend!"

They piled out of the car, and the man walked over to them. He was dressed in a pair of ragged overalls and had beads of sweat dancing on his forehead. "You're late."

"So sorry," Isabella apologized. "Charles? Good to meet you. Sorry we are late. We hit some traffic outside of Eugene."

He eyed her suspiciously. "There usually isn't traffic outside of Eugene."

"There was today," Tiffany chimed in.

He peered at them. He appeared to be in his late fifties, and Tracy was taken aback by the look of contempt on his face.

"You're here for the party?" he asked. "I have never heard of anyone planning a party in Greenhithe Falls before..."

Isabella laughed, but Tracy realized the man wasn't joking. "It's the wine capital of the region," Isabella reminded him. "I read online that there are vineyards, boutique shops, and restaurants galore around here. Tracy, our bride, is a low-key gal, and I knew this would be the perfect place to celebrate her!"

Charles blinked. "I think you have the wrong Greenhithe Falls."

Isabella laughed again. "You are a scream," she praised him. "Such a character. Can you help us get the bags inside? Thank you again for letting us rent the house. This will be the perfect place for our trip."

He said nothing but reached down and took two bags from the pile. "Follow me."

As they followed him inside of the house, past the pig pens and cow barn, Tracy had a sinking feeling that Isabella had made a grave mistake.

"But... but... I don't understand," Isabella said in confusion as she looked at the map Charles was showing them. "Where are the wineries? What about the Michelin star farm to table restaurant? I thought the shops and art galleries were downtown, too."

Charles shook his head. "I think you have the wrong Greenhithe Falls," he explained gruffly as Isabella's face fell. "You are thinking of Greenhouse Falls, the resort town in Northern California. This is Green*hithe* Falls, a rural farm community. People used to mistake the two all the time in the age before the internet... I guess you just didn't do a lot of research before you booked with us."

Tracy's mouth felt dry as she saw Isabella's eyes flash with rage. "Why didn't you say something when I booked the house?" she asked Charles. "In my email, I mentioned that I was looking forward to a fun girls weekend with a bride to be! Why didn't you realize what I had done?"

Charles crossed his arms over his chest. "It ain't my job to fix tourists' mistakes," he scoffed. "I have enough to do around the farm without worrying about silly city girls trooping out here to party."

Rose smiled kindly. "Look, we've clearly made a mistake. Is there any way we can get a refund? We'll just take our things and get out of your hair…."

"No refunds," he stated. "The policy is firm."

"What about a partial refund?" Rose pushed, using her sweetest voice as she coaxed the grumpy farmer.

"No refunds."

Isabella looked shellshocked. "Well, then this is it, I guess…"

"Happy bachelorette weekend to me," Tracy sarcastically thought to herself as she sat down on the blue and white plaid couch.

Charles led them around the interior of the blue house. It was small and quaint, with rustic decor and shabby wood floors. It was clean though, and as Charles gave them their tour, she claimed the bedroom with the king-size bed.

They all returned downstairs, and Charles gave them a huge brass key. "That is the only key that works for the front door," he told them. "Be careful, though. The front steps are a little wobbly, and you need to watch your step."

"Are you taking notes?" Isabella snapped sarcastically to Tiffany. "No boutiques, no restaurants, and the front step is wobbly."

Charles shot her a look. "This is *my* family's farm, and the property *will* be respected," he insisted as they gathered in the kitchen. He held up a binder. "These are the house rules."

Tracy opened it and read the first page. "No parties, no gum, no smoking, no feathers, no glitter, no loud music after seven, no guests, no littering, and swimming on the property pond is only permitted between the hours of 1p-2p."

"That's a lot of rules," Tiffany commented.

"This property has been in our family for a century," Charles explained. "It's a lavender farm, like the other farms around here. We rent out this house for some extra income, but we expect all guests to treat it like it was their own."

Charles turned swiftly and coughed into his shoulder. "'Scuse me," he pardoned himself after hacking for nearly a minute.

"Do you need a cough drop?" Rose offered. "I have some in my purse."

He took out a worn handkerchief from his pocket and blew his nose. "Cough drops are for sissies," he countered as he stuffed the used handkerchief back into his pocket. "I'm fine."

Before Rose could respond, he pounded his chest with his fist. "See? Healthy as a horse."

Tracy stared at him. "You don't sound like it…"

"I'm fine," he snapped. "Look, do you all need anything else? I need to get back to work…"

Rose shook her head. "I think we will be just fine," she assured him. "Your property is so… quiet! We are so happy to be here."

"Good," he nodded. "Oh, one last thing. Tomorrow, my youngest sister, Holly, would like to host you all for breakfast. We don't usually offer food to guests, but when she read your email, she insisted. She's young and doesn't get a lot of female company around here, and she's looking forward to having you at our table."

"No, that's okay-" Isabella started, but Tracy cut her off.

"The more the merrier." She smiled weakly. "We can't wait to meet her."

"And be *nice*," Tracy urged Isabella as the group shuffled over to the main house for breakfast the next morning. "It isn't their fault that…"

"That what?" Isabella snapped. "That I didn't book the right place? That I got us stuck in this farm town? That I ruined your bachelorette trip?"

"I didn't say that," Tracy responded coolly.

Rose piped in. "It's a lovely morning, the sun is shining, and a nice breakfast awaits us," she told them. "This isn't what we expected, but we are going to have a lovely time. We can take long walks around the property, play some games, and just enjoy the peace and quiet."

"Yeah! Tracy, trust me, this is way better than Vegas," Tiffany chimed in. "No loud clubs, no scantily clad waitresses offering bottle service, and no busy restaurants teeming with people."

Tracy imagined her fiance being served cocktails at a club and shuddered. "Yeah, this is way better," she forced herself to agree as she looked around the large yard.

They knocked on the door of the main house, expecting Charles to answer. Instead, a young, pretty woman dressed in jeans and a white sleeveless button-up shirt greeted them.

"The bachelorette party," she squealed in excitement. "I'm Holly. Welcome to our home. Come in, come in!"

Holly had brown bangs and a long braid down her back. Her green eyes sparkled with joy, and she beckoned them into the dining room. A long oak table was piled high with home cooked dishes, including eggs benedicts, French toast, and breakfast casserole. "Sit, sit!"

The women sat down at the table.

"It looks amazing," Tiffany swooned. "Are those homemade cinnamon rolls?"

"You bet," Holly grinned. "Please, dig in. Help yourself to whatever you would like. When Charles mentioned a group of ladies was coming to stay, I got so excited. I started cooking and just didn't stop."

They filled their plates and chatted with Holly over the delicious meal. Tracy could tell Holly and Charles were siblings by their angular chins and tall stature, but in personality, they were totally different. While Charles was grumpy and standoffish, Holly was chatty and hospitable. She asked them all about their families, their lives, and told them everything they could ever want to know about the history of the lavender farm.

"Our great-grandaddy settled here after he lost his sons and wife on the Oregon Trail," Holly told them. "He had to start over. He built the house where you are staying and then met my great-grandmama, Fern. They had a son, my granddaddy, and then built this very house where we are sitting right now!"

"What a story," Rose mused. "How lovely that you know so much about your family history."

"We are a very proud family," Holly smiled. "This farm grew beyond my great-grandaddy's wildest dreams, and now, it is our job to continue his legacy. Before he passed, my brothers and I promised our daddy that we would take care of the land and the farm, and here we are!"

"Brothers?" Isabella asked as she perked up. "You have more brothers around?"

Holly laughed. "Oh, yes. And a sister! You met Charles, of course. He's an old grouch, but he is a hard worker and makes sure this place gets by. Derrick and Abraham are ten years younger than him, and they live on the property with their families. Molly is five years older than me, and she is around, too."

"And you?" Rose asked. "What about you?"

"I'm the youngest by over a decade," Holly explained. "Our parents didn't plan to have five children, but sometimes, life works out differently than planned. They died when I was a girl, and Charles and the other boys and Molly raised me here."

Tracy raised an eyebrow. "Speaking of Charles, is he coming to breakfast?"

Before Holly could answer, they heard shouting from outside.

"What's going on?" Tiffany asked. "Are those the animals?"

Isabella shot her a look. "Animals can't scream, Tiffany…"

Holly's eyes widened. "That sounds like Derrick," she muttered. "Excuse me, ladies. I need to pop outside and see what's going on."

She stood up and hastily pushed in her chair before running out the back door. As the door slammed behind her, the sound of an ambulance filled the air.

"What is going on?" Tracy asked.

"We should go see," Tiffany decided. "Let's go."

They left the table and hurried outside, where they saw Holly crouched on the ground.

"Oh my gosh," Rose shuddered. "Is that…"

Tracy saw Charles lying in his sister's arms. He was foaming at the mouth, and she watched as his chest heaved up and down as he gasped for breath.

Charles reached up and grabbed for his own throat. His eyes looked like they were going to bulge out of his head as he clawed at his throat.

Charles began to convulse. His eyes rolled back in his head, and his body shuddered violently as Holly tried to pin him down. She was using her body weight to hold his arms by his sides.

"Help me!" she wailed as Rose and Tracy hurried over to her side.

"What happened?" Tracy asked as she looked at Charles' shaking body. "Does he need CPR?"

"I don't think it's safe to do that right now," Rose commented, observing his jerky movements. "Holly, it looks like he is having a seizure. We should roll him onto his side."

Holly's face turned pale. "Can that happen?"

With a thud, Charles' legs gave a final kick before he went completely still. His eyes looked right at Tracy, sending a chill down her spine.

Out of nowhere, a tall, muscular man in a plaid shirt hurried over and sat beside them, and a shorter man with a baseball cap was waving an ambulance over from the driveway.

"Charles," Holly sobbed as she buried her face in his shirt. "Charles! Wake up, Charles. Please, wake up."

Tracy gaped at her. "What's wrong with him?"

No one answered her, and she stepped out of the way as three EMTs pushed a gurney past her. They examined Charles, and then one of the EMTs went back to the ambulance, returning a moment later with a thin blue sheet. She covered Charles with it, and they loaded him onto the gurney and into the ambulance.

Another wail of sirens filled the air, and Tracy turned to see a police car coasting down the long dirt driveway.

"What is going on?" Isabella hissed.

"I think he's *dead*, Is," Tracy told her friend. "I think Charles Walker is dead."

5

olly wept as one of the men—presumably her brother—tried to pull her to her feet. She collapsed again, and the EMTs took her pulse.

The police car parked next to the house. Two officers emerged. Tracy noticed that while they were wearing typical police officer uniforms, they also wore white cowboy hats and boots.

"Hey, y'all," the shorter officer greeted them. "We heard there was some trouble on Walker Farm. What's going on?"

"Marty," Holly cried as the officer bent down next to her. "He's dead! Charles is dead."

The officers looked stunned. "Dead?" the other officer asked. "Charles? What happened?"

The man in the baseball cap looked down at his brown work boots. "I found him in the barn," he shared. "I came out to check on the calves, and Charles was lying on the ground. He was covered in vomit."

"Was he drunk again, Derrick?" the taller officer asked. "Sounds like Charles…"

"I don't know," Derrick lamented. "He really cut down on the drinking after his last checkup. I don't think he was sitting in the barn alone drinking himself to death."

The muscular man shook his head. "Heart problems?" he suggested. "I was born with a heart murmur, and so was Charles."

"Yeah, Abraham, I didn't think about that," Derrick agreed. "Or he worked himself to death? You know how Charles was. Holly, what do you think?"

Tracy could see that the youngest Walker was inconsolable and could barely speak. "I… I… I…"

Abraham put a hand on her shoulder. "She's so upset," he commented as the police officers gave them looks of sympathy.

The four out-of-towners turned to each other. "Maybe we should just go," Isabella suggested. "This seems to be out of hand, and I think we are in the way."

"I agree," Rose nodded. "We'll tell the police we arrived last night and have no idea what's happening, and then we'll be on our way."

Tracy agreed, but before she could speak up, Holly interrupted them.

"Hey," she sniffled. "I am so sorry for the chaos. As you can see, we are in the midst of a family crisis, and I am so sorry you had to see it all play out."

Tracy smiled kindly. "We are so sorry for your loss," she said as she reached out to touch Holly's arm. "We are going to chat with the officers and get out of your way. We don't want to add to your distress."

Holly nodded. "Thanks, ladies," she said softly. "We'll talk soon."

The women returned to the guest house. They sat in silence for nearly forty-five minutes, not knowing what to say after such a traumatic experience. Finally, Rose piped up.

"Hey," she said quietly, a small smile on her face. "I know this is a rough situation, but things have to get better from here, right?"

Tiffany bit her lip. "I don't know. This whole time has been weird," she replied as Isabella glared daggers at her.

"Is that supposed to be a dig at me?" she hissed as Tiffany's eyes widened.

"What? I didn't say anything about you," Tiffany snapped back, standing up and putting her hands on her hips.

Isabella's eyes narrowed as she rose to her feet and moved to stand in front of Tiffany. "Look, I did my best to plan this weekend, okay?! It's not like I meant to stick us out in the middle of nowhere, and it's not like I knew that old guy was going to die!"

Tiffany shook her head. "I wasn't even talking about you," she countered. "You always manage to make everything about yourself."

Isabella whirled around to look at Tracy. "You don't believe that, do you?" she asked, her voice growing higher pitched. "Tracy, tell her she's wrong. I can't believe she's targeting me like this."

Tracy peeked over at her aunt. Rose bit her lip.

"Tracy?" Isabella demanded. "Tell Tiffany she is being unreasonable. This is your party, and you shouldn't let her speak to me like this."

Rose interjected, holding up her hands to silence them. "Girls, sit down," she urged them. "Stop. Let's all chat for a moment."

Isabella huffed as she sat down on the couch. Tiffany curled up on the floor with her legs crossed, leaning her elbow on her knee.

"I remember a bachelorette party I went to for my cousin, Gina," she told them as she sat back down. "Back in my day, these little gatherings were so much simpler; we typically only went out for a night or so, and even those outings were quiet and low-key."

Isabella raised an eyebrow. "What does that have to do with this mess?" she asked.

Rose playfully put her pointer finger in front of her lips to silence her. "Shush! Just listen."

She leaned back and rested her arms against the back of the couch. "Anyway, back to my story. At Gina's party, we had a little hiccup. We were driving to a dance club in the city when Gina's sister's car broke down on the side of the road. We didn't have car services back then, so we thought we were out of luck."

Tiffany cocked her head to the side. "So, what did you do? Did you get to go dancing?"

Rose shrugged. "We were really disappointed," she shared. "Gina had been looking forward to her night of dancing, and we were all dressed up and ready to go."

Isabella wrinkled her nose. "What does that have to do with this situation?"

Rose winked. "Just listen," she urged. "Gina's sister was devastated that the fabulous night out she had planned for her sister was ruined. We were stuck on the side of the road for two hours until a good Samaritan stopped to help us. He was tall and handsome, and it turns out that the car breaking down was fate. Gina's sister married him six months later, and they are still married to this day. I have their last holiday card on my refrigerator, in fact."

Tiffany blinked. "I don't get it."

Rose sighed. "Sometimes, the worst situations can result in amazing outcomes," she explained.

Isabella shook her head. "I don't know if some old dude dying at Tracy's bachelorette party can lead to anything amazing," she commented.

"I think what Aunt Rose is saying is that things may not always be as bad as they first appear," Tiffany said.

"Exactly!" Rose exclaimed. "I'm sure the police will soon give us a logical explanation for what happened, apologize for any inconvenience we may have experienced and help us turn our lemons into lemonade," she continued, hoping to lift the spirits of the younger ladies.

Tracy exhaled loudly. "I'm surprised the police haven't been over here to talk with us," she said, looking left and then right as if they were going to bust in at that moment. "Do you think Holly will have to give them our information?"

As if it had been planned, there was a loud knock on the front door. Tiffany answered it, and she nervously returned to the living room of the guest house. "It's the police."

Two officers appeared. "I'm Marty, and this is my partner, Robin," the male officer introduced as the women stared at them. "We have some questions for you."

"Questions?" Isabella asked. "What kinds of questions? I am not going to answer a thing until my lawyer is present. I have rights, you know."

Marty and Robin turned to give each other a look.

"What do you need to know?" Tracy offered, trying to be helpful.

"Were you ladies here when Charles Walker passed away?" Robin asked, her dark eyes filled with suspicion as she looked at their faces.

"Yes," Tiffany answered, and Isabella kicked her ankle. "Well, not where he died, but we were on the property."

Robin took a note in a yellow notepad that she retrieved from her belt

"So you four women were with Charles on his last night alive?" he asked. "Good to know. Well ladies, make yourselves at home. No one is leaving this farm until we have the answers we need."

"The answers?" Tiffany asked. "Answers to what?"

Robin stared at her. "Given the information and the state of Charles Walker's body, we are declaring this death a homicide," she shared. "The four of you met him and interacted with him yesterday, which leads me to believe that one of you knows something."

"What?" Tracy cried. "We don't know anything! We only spoke to him for ten minutes or so."

Marty put his hands on his waist. "I think I was clear," he warned her. "None of you are leaving until we figure out who killed Charles Walker, and that's that!"

6

Tracy barely slept that night. She tossed and turned as horrible dreams plagued her, and she felt uneasy when she finally decided to give up on sleep and start the day.

She rubbed her eyes as she stumbled out of the bedroom she had to herself. Aunt Rose, Isabella, and Tiffany were sharing the spacious bunk room next door to her room, and she tiptoed, trying not to wake anyone.

The sun had not yet risen, and the sky was an ominous shade of gray as Tracy searched through the rustic wood cabinets for coffee filters. She yawned, and the abrupt cackle of a rooster crowing in the distance nearly made her jump out of her own skin.

"Ugh," she groaned, hoping the other women would sleep through the noise. Tracy needed some time to herself, and she envisioned a quiet half hour on the porch sipping her coffee as the sun came up over the fields.

"Hi! You're up early."

Tracy heard Tiffany's voice booming from the hallway before the girl had even entered the kitchen.

"So are you," she commented, not trying to hide the annoyance in her voice.

Tiffany cheerfully grinned at her. "I slept like a rock," she shared. "I don't know if it's the fresh country air or the mattress in the bunk room, but whatever it is, it was magical."

"That's nice," Tracy said flatly as she added water to the coffeemaker.

She heard someone padding down the hallway and sighed. Her dreams of a quiet morning were officially dashed.

"Good morning," Isabella greeted them as she strode into the kitchen in her matching navy silk slippers and robe. "Is there coffee?"

Tracy gestured at the coffeemaker. "Almost done."

Isabella wrinkled her nose. "Oh. That isn't quite what I meant."

Tiffany lifted her left eyebrow. "What?"

Isabella fluttered her eyelashes. "An organic pour over with oat milk and just a tiny bit of agave?"

Tracy laughed in spite of herself. "In your dreams, princess. We're on the farm, Isabella. What you see is what you get out here, and what you are seeing is a pot of store-bought coffee. We might have some 2% milk in the refrigerator, if I remember correctly."

Her friend's eyes widened in horror. *"Milk?* With lactose? Like, from a *cow?"*

"That's how I drank it as a girl, and I turned out just fine," Rose assured Isabella as she bustled into the room. "Good morning, girls," she smiled as she planted a kiss on Tracy's forehead. "Tracy, did you sleep well?"

"Not really," Tracy grumbled, but before Rose could respond, there was a knock on the front door.

"Who could that be at this hour?" Tiffany wondered aloud. "Do you think the police are back to ask us more questions?"

"I hope not," Isabella sighed. "They kept us up late enough with their questions and prodding. I need a break."

Tiffany went to answer the door and returned with Holly Walker. Holly was dressed in a clean pair of dark wash jeans, a long-sleeve floral henley shirt buttoned up to her collarbone, and a sweatshirt tied around her waist. Despite her tidy outfit, Tracy noticed her eyes were bloodshot and her face was pale. Her hair was pulled up in a messy bun, and she was not wearing earrings.

"Hey, girls," she waved. "How did you all sleep?"

"Great," everyone except for Tracy assured her.

"How are *you*, honey?" Rose asked softly. "You've been through so much in the last day. I am so sorry for your loss."

"Thanks," Holly shrugged, looking down at her brown boots. "I can't believe he's gone. I think I am in shock, though. I'm trying my best to distract myself."

"That's a very natural instinct," Rose promised her, wrapping her arm around Holly's shoulder in a maternal way.

"Sometimes, our minds are not ready to process what our hearts know is true."

Holly nodded. "That sounds right…"

Tracy blinked. "Did the police have any new information?" she asked.

"Tracy!" Isabella hissed at her. "Leave the girl alone. She's exhausted and doesn't need an interrogation from us. We're probably stressing her and her family out just by being around."

"Sorry," Tracy apologized.

Holly smiled softly. "Actually, I'm glad you all stayed," she declared. "You will be such a nice distraction for our family. In fact, I wanted to come see if you all would help me with something this morning."

Rose nodded earnestly. "Anything!"

"With my brother gone, I will need some help with the chores around here," she explained. "I need help feeding the cows in the big barn up the hill. Would you all have any interest in helping? It's an easy job and the cows are so sweet."

Tracy and Rose nodded in unison, but Tiffany and Isabella said nothing.

"Is that a yes?" Holly coaxed. "It would mean a lot to me."

Tiffany started to bite her nails. "I'm not sure I'm good with animals," she muttered.

"I don't eat meat," Isabella added.

Holly giggled. "I'm asking you to *feed* the cows, not *eat* them!"

Tracy shot Isabella a look.

"Okay," Isabella finally agreed. "We'll help you."

The next hour was spent treading through the enormous barn and placing piles and piles of hay in each stall as the cows mooed gratefully.

"We usually have the cows out in the pasture to eat and play and live their best lives, but this herd has been sick this week," Holly told them. "We are keeping a special eye on them and hope to have them back out in their happy place early next week."

Tracy noticed Isabella stifling a gag. "It's not that bad," she told her friend. "And look, some of the cows have little babies with them."

Tracy crouched down in front of a stall and reached her hand inside to stroke the forehead of a bulky brown cow. "You sure are a big cow," she whispered as the cow slobbered over her hand. "And a sweet one too!"

The cow made a noise, and Holly grinned in approval. "That cow really likes you, Tracy. You seem to be a natural with animals."

She smiled. "These cows are so sweet."

Holly pointed at the cow's large stomach. "She's due any day now."

"She's pregnant?"

Holly's face glowed with excitement. "We think she might be having a very large calf."

Tracy felt a tugging sensation in her heart as she surveyed the heavily pregnant cow. She placed a hand on her stomach and closed her eyes, imagining what it would be like to have her own children someday. She was nearly a married woman, and as Tracy pictured her life with Warren, she wondered if perhaps the very best was still to come.

7

O ut of the blue, the cow in the stall behind Tracy relieved itself. Tiffany started laughing at the sight and smell, but Tracy's stomach lurched as the stench flooded her nostrils.

"I need to step out," she apologized, throwing her hand over her mouth and hurrying out of the barn.

She gasped as she hurled herself outside, breathing deeply in through her nostrils and out of her mouth.

"What's the matter with you? Too much to drink?" a man's voice laughed as Tracy bent over and placed her hands on her knees.

"Weak stomach," she groaned as she slowly stood back up and turned to face the man.

It was clear the man was a Walker; he looked just like a younger, stronger version of Charles. He was dressed in a pair of jeans, dirt-stained boots, and a Carhartt jacket.

"You aren't from around here, are you?" he asked, eyeing her mud-splattered white sneakers, Lilly Pulitzer rain jacket, and pearl earrings. "I'm surprised my sister didn't send your party home after—"

She watched as he hung his head.

"I'm so sorry for your loss," she offered, noticing the man's lower lip was quivering.

He took a long breath before looking up at her. "Thanks," he whispered. "I miss him so much already, but on the farm, life has to go on. Seeing new animals born, crops growing, and livestock sent off to the slaughter is a constant reminder of the circle of life."

"That's a poetic way to consider it," she offered kindly.

"It's just facts," he stated before extending his dirty hand to shake hers. "I'm Derrick, by the way. Derrick Walker."

"I figured," she told him. "You look just like-"

She stopped as she watched his face flood with grief.

"Just like Charles, huh? I know, I know. Everyone has always said I was practically his twin. I loved following him around when I was a kid; I thought Charles hung the stars in the sky."

She nodded sympathetically. "It's so nice that you two stayed close."

Tracy saw his nostrils begin to flare.

"Yeah, *close*," he muttered as his brows knit together. "As close as you can be with an alcoholic."

"What?" she asked. "What do you mean?"

Derrick scowled. "Look, I loved my brother, and I will miss him until my heart stops beating, but Charlie wasn't an angel. He had his demons."

"His demons?" Tracy inquired, peering into Derrick's sad eyes. "What do you mean?"

She noticed his body began to tense up, and Tracy saw Derrick ball his large, dirty hands into fists.

"He got what was coming to him," he finally replied in a gruff voice. "Charles got what he deserved. It's time we all got over it and just moved on."

He turned on his heel and stormed away, leaving Tracy all alone with a million questions dancing through her mind. What did Derrick mean when he said that Charles got what he deserved? He seemed distraught, but did he know more than he was letting on?

* * *

"IT SOUNDS like he just drank himself to death," Tiffany speculated as the ladies relaxed on the back porch of the guest house that afternoon. "It sounds like he had some serious issues."

Rose frowned. "We barely know these people," she chided Tiffany, giving her a soft swat on the knee as she sat beside her on the wooden porch swing. "I don't think it is in good taste to make assumptions like that."

"I'm drawing conclusions from what *they* said," the young woman insisted, crossing her arms over her chest. "I'm not trying to be rude."

Isabella was sitting on the ledge of the porch with a nail file in her hands. She was studying her manicured fingers with an angry look on her face.

"I guess my manicure was for nothing," she grumbled as she moved the nail file like a saw across her thumbnail. "I didn't sign up for a weekend of manual labor. I should send the Walker family an invoice for these ruined nails."

Tracy sighed, leaning against the porch.

"What?" Tiffany asked her. "What was that for?"

"What was what for?" Tracy replied, feeling a dull headache begin to creep in.

"That sigh. Why did you sigh like that?"

Tracy exhaled. "I just wish we could talk about something else."

Isabella nodded. "I second that. We should be talking about *Tracy* and her wedding. It's her bachelorette weekend, after all."

"You're right," Rose agreed. "The Walker family's loss is a tragedy, but the weekend must go on. You know, when my darling Frank passed, I found great comfort in distracting myself and focusing on other things. Perhaps we can include Holly in a few of our activities to help distract her!"

"That would be so nice," Tiffany chimed in. "Holly can join us for some of our games and fun. Is that okay, Tracy?"

Tracy gave a weak smile. "Sure," she said softly. "No problem."

Isabella stood up and brushed off her beige linen pants. "I'm going to go inside and get ready," she announced. "It's time to kick the weekend off the *right* way!"

8

"It's a bummer Holly couldn't join us," Tiffany complained as they drove down a long gravel driveway.

"She's helping with funeral arrangements, Tiff," Tracy reminded her. "I'm sure we'll see more of her later."

Isabella parked the car. "We're here, ladies!"

The women exited the vehicle and stood outside of a small tin shack on the outskirts of town. The shack was located right next to a small pond, and a narrow wooden dock jutted out into the yellow-green water. Isabella clapped her hands with excitement, though Tracy could see her friend's smile was not real. Isabella's eyes were filled with concern as she surveyed the shack.

Tiffany scrunched up her nose. "We aren't going in that water, are we, Isabella? Is this a swimming excursion?"

Isabella shook her head. "No, silly," she laughed. "We're going over to the dock! I did a little research, and this is one of the prettiest spots in town to take photos. I thought we could snap some fun pictures for Tracy to post on her Facebook page."

Tracy raised an eyebrow. "This is a *photoshoot?*"

Isabella pulled a tripod out of her giant Gucci purse. "Don't you want some cute pictures to make Warren wish he were here instead of out partying with the boys in Vegas?"

Tracy's face fell. She hadn't heard from her fiance all day, and she was both annoyed about his silence *and* worried about him.

"Fine," she agreed. "I wish you had told me, though. I would have worked a little harder on my makeup."

Before Isabella could reply, a woman in patched overalls marched out of the shack.

"Are y'all here to fish?" she asked, placing her hands on her hips and staring at them intently. "We charge extra for groups bigger than two, you know."

Isabella shook her head. "No," she told the woman. "We're here for a bachelorette party. We wanted to take some photos on the dock."

The woman scowled. "This is private property," she hissed. "You can't just come in here and use my dock without permission."

"Okay," Isabella nodded. "May we use the dock for a few minutes?"

The woman eyed their group. "I ain't hosting no photoshoot," she refused. "This is a pond for *fishing*. Either you pay the group rate for a fishing day on the pond or leave."

Rose smiled sweetly. "We'll do it," she decided as Isabella's jaw dropped. "Come on, girls! We can take photos anywhere. Let's have an adventure. Tracy? What do you think?"

Tracy bit her lip. She had not been thrilled with the prospect of a makeshift photoshoot, but the idea of fishing on the stinky pond didn't sound ideal, either. Still, she wanted to be kind and flexible, so she gave a small nod. "Fine."

"That'll be one-hundred dollars for the group," the woman informed them. "Cash only."

Isabella's eyes widened. "I don't have cash," she protested. "I only use my credit card. I want to get points."

Rose and Tiffany reached into their pockets and pulled out a few crumbled bills.

"Would you take seventy-five?" Rose asked earnestly. "Please? It's Tracy's bachelorette party, and this would be so fun for her."

The woman furrowed her brow, but finally, she nodded. "Fine," she agreed. "Seventy-five. That includes your gear and the poles."

"Great!" Rose grinned. "Thank you so much."

The woman turned on her heel. "I'll get the stuff," she huffed as she walked back toward the shack. "Wait here."

Isabella looked worried. "Are we sure we want to do this?" she asked as she glanced around the property. "The water isn't so clean, and it's really smelly out here. I'm being eaten alive by the bugs, too."

Rose held her head high. "This weekend is about Tracy," she said firmly. "And this will be a fun activity for her party. We will make the most of it."

"I used to fish all the time when I was little," Tiffany chimed in eagerly. "It'll be fun, Bells. You'll love it!"

Moments later, the woman returned with four fishing poles, a bucket, and a lidded white container.

"Here," she said as she shoved the poles into Tiffany's arms. "And take this."

She gave the container to Isabella.

"What's this?" Isabella asked, raising her eyebrow as she held the container. "Gloves? Hand sanitizer?"

"Bait," the woman explained. "It's bait."

Tracy looked at her aunt. "Bait?"

"Worms!" Tiffany giggled. "It's a bowl of worms."

Isabella screamed as she threw the container down to the ground. The lid popped off, and dozens of small, wriggling worms spilled out onto the dock.

"What did you do that for?" the woman shrieked. "Now they are everywhere. Pick them up before they crawl away!"

Isabella stomped her feet. "Pick them up? Worms? Ewwwwww!!"

The old woman bent down and reached for the worms with her bare hands. She stuffed them back into the container and closed the lid over it, accidentally crushing a worm in the process. Its limp body hung outside of the container, leaving a pale brown stain on the vessel.

"Take it," the woman urged Isabella. "Don't drop it again, or I'll charge you extra."

Tiffany reached for the container. "Thanks," she smiled. "Let's go, girls!"

The worm fiasco was only the tip of the iceberg for the group; Isabella refused to touch her fishing pole, Tracy could not bring herself to thread her hook through a live worm, and Rose's line snapped as soon as she cast it out. Tiffany was the only one with some success; while the others struggled, she caught two massive bluegills in a row.

"Look at his scales," she beamed as she pulled her second fish out of the water. "That green and yellow color is gorgeous. Isabella, do you want to see?"

Isabella shook her hand. "Absolutely not."

Tiffany held the flopping fish in front of Tracy's face. "What do you think?"

Tracy felt squeamish at the live fish gasping for breath. "It's… nice."

Tiffany plopped the fish into her bucket. She plucked a new worm out of the container and pierced its squirming body with her hook. "Let's see if I can snag a third fish. If I catch a few more, we can make dinner for ourselves back at the house!"

Rose sighed. "I wish my line hadn't snapped," she fretted. "I used to go fishing with Frank and loved it."

"Take my pole," Isabella urged her. "Please. I'm not going to need it."

The women turned around at the sound of heavy footsteps from behind them. "Hey," a man's voice called out. "Do y'all need some help? I heard a line snapped?"

He looked to be around Tiffany's age and was wearing ripped jeans and a faded baseball cap. "Mama said y'all were out here, and I wanted to check on you," he smiled. "She can be a bit of a handful, but her bark is worse than her bite."

"You live here?" Rose asked politely.

Tiffany batted her eyelashes. "That was your mom? She was so funny."

"Funny? I don't hear that often about her, but that's good to hear. I live in town, but I come out to check on Mama every afternoon," he explained. "She hasn't been the same since my dad passed."

Rose gave him a sympathetic look. "I am so sorry," she told him.

"Me too," Tiffany added, clearly smitten with the young man.

"Thanks, but he passed away ten years ago. At some point, she has to move on," he shrugged.

His comment reminded Tracy of Derrick's insistence on the Walker family moving forward after Charles' death. She shivered, thinking of the dark look in his eyes.

"Here, let me help you," the young man offered as he carefully took Rose's pole. "I'll get you gals squared away so you can all catch something."

He fixed her pole and moved onto Tracy. "Scared of the worms?" he asked kindly as she nodded.

Without a word, he selected a thick, pink worm from the container and looped the hook through its belly.

He turned to Tiffany and peeked into her bucket. "You are a natural," he praised her. "You don't need my help."

"She does," Tiffany chuckled as she gestured at Isabella.

"I don't need any help," Isabella insisted in a prissy voice. "I just want to watch."

The young man cocked his head to the side. "You don't like fishing?"

"I don't care for it," Isabella answered primly before beginning to stare at the man's biceps that were bulging out of his flannel shirt. "Then again…. maybe you could teach me a thing or two?"

"I would like that," he winked at her before turning to the other three women. "Y'all ain't from around here, are you?"

"We're from out of town," Tiffany said quickly. Tracy noticed her friend was blushing. "We're here celebrating Tracy's bachelorette party."

"Awww. Congratulations, ma'am," he nodded at Tracy. "So you're spending your big weekend with the girls at our little pond?"

Rose patted Tracy's back. "Tracy is a low-maintenance, go-with-the-flow kind of girl," she praised her niece. "We've had a few bumps during this weekend, but she's been a champ."

He looked over at Isabella. "Fishing is real fun, but are you all planning to go out while you are here?" he asked hopefully. "Do some partying?"

Isabella's eyes lit up at the attention. The young man clearly was not her type, but Tracy knew her friend adored being flirted with by anyone. "Partying? Is there a place to party here?"

He threw his head back and laughed. "What, you don't think farmers and hicks know how to have fun? Y'all should come out. The country bar is having live music tonight. It'll be fun."

"Live music?" Tiffany asked, putting her hand on the guy's shoulder. "That would be a blast."

His eyes were fixed on Isabella. "So y'all will come?"

She smirked. "We'll be there."

Isabella and the young man exchanged information before he walked away. "See y'all later," he called out. "And maybe we can arrange that little fishing lesson for tomorrow?"

"If you're lucky," Isabella called out in a sultry voice.

Tiffany stuck out her lower lip. "It isn't fair," she pouted as he disappeared into the shack. "You don't even like fishing and the hot fishing guy flirts with *you*?!"

Isabella tossed her hair. "It's about confidence, Tiffany," she shrugged. "And who knows? Maybe you'll meet someone at the bar tonight."

Tiffany put her hands on her hips. "I don't wanna meet someone," she countered. "I wanted to talk to *him.*"

Isabella winked at her. "Remember, dear, there are *always* more fish in the sea."

9

Tracy felt beautiful as she studied her appearance in the floor-length mirror in her bedroom. Her hair was pulled back into a high, sleek bun, and she wore red lipstick that made her feel sexy and mysterious. She was wearing an outfit that was a tad outside of her comfort zone, but she felt every bit the part of a bride-to-be on her bachelorette party in her cropped white puff sleeved top that showed just a tiny sliver of her midriff and an A-line sequin white skirt with fringe at the bottom.

She walked into the hallway and Rose applauded. "You look beautiful," she complimented Tracy. "That skirt and top are just adorable."

"Do you think this is too much?" Isabella asked as she strutted out of the bunkroom in a white miniskirt, a pearl-encrusted headband, and a cream bandeau top.

"You look… festive," Rose told her as she eyed the skimpy outfit.

Isabella did a twirl. "The skirt is new," she grinned, reaching a hand up to smooth her hair. "I think it makes my legs look a million miles long."

Tracy cleared her throat. "You look like a model, as you always do," she told her friend. "But there is a problem with your outfit."

Isabella's eyes grew large with concern. "What? Is the cream and white combination not working? I love pairing neutrals and thought it looked posh."

Tiffany, who was dressed in a green sleeveless shift dress and wedge sandals, shook her head. "Isabella, that's not what Tracy means."

"What is the problem?" Isabella wondered. "Is the skirt too short?"

Tracy stared at her friend. "It's my *bachelorette* party, Isabella," she explained slowly, trying not to lose her cool. "You're practically wearing all white."

"What? No, I am not," Isabella replied, her voice tinged with confusion. "Tracy, this top is *cream*. That isn't even close to white."

"The skirt is white," Tracy said flatly. "Come on, Isabella. Can you please change?"

Isabella glowered at her. "Are you serious? You're asking me to change my outfit?"

Rose put a hand on Isabella's shoulder. "Sweetie, come on," she urged her. "It's Tracy's weekend."

Isabella looked at Tiffany. "And you agree with this?"

Tiffany nodded. "It's her bachelorette weekend," she repeated. "How would you feel if Tracy wore that to your party?"

Tracy felt the heat rising in her cheeks as Isabella stormed out of the room.

"What is her problem?" she asked Tiffany. "It's like she doesn't even remember that I am the one who is getting married."

Rose exhaled. "I think she's a little envious, honey," she advised her niece. "And a little embarrassed that her grand plans for the weekend didn't live up to what she expected."

Before Tracy could reply, Isabella reappeared in a black romper with five-inch-high heels and a red scarf tied fashionably around her neck. "Is this better?"

"It's perfect," Tracy told her, hoping to avoid drama. "Let's get out of here. Aunt Rose, are you driving?"

Rose tossed the car keys to Tiffany. "I am tuckered out, girls," she yawned. "I am going to hit the hay early. You all have fun! Call me if you need anything."

"What? Come on, Rose," Tiffany pleaded. "Come with us. I need a wingwoman."

Rose giggled. "A wingwoman?"

Tiffany smiled. "Someone to help me meet guys. Isabella will be too busy with that cute fishing guy, and Tracy is getting married, so I need your help."

Rose shook her head. "I think I will have to pass," she told her. "You will have so much fun *celebrating Tracy* for *her* party."

Tracy appreciated the emphasis her aunt had put on reminding the girls that it was her special weekend.

"We'll see you later, then," Tiffany waved as she walked out the door.

"Toodles," Isabella blew a kiss to Rose.

Tracy leaned down to kiss her aunt goodbye. "I'll miss you," she murmured as she embraced her. "Those two are on the prowl, it seems."

Rose looked into Tracy's eyes. "It isn't fun being out with single friends," she admitted. "But remember, dear, you are marrying an amazing man. They might have fun flirting and batting their eyelashes, but you have something *real* with Warren."

"Then why haven't I heard from him?" Tracy wondered as she stood up and smoothed her skirt.

The bar was dark and loud, with high top tables clustered in the corner and a huge wooden stage in the center of the room where a young woman in white cowgirl boots and a short yellow dress played guitar and sang.

"Let's get a table," Isabella suggested as they walked by the bar. "I wonder if they do bottle service here."

"I don't think that's an option," Tracy laughed in spite of herself as a waitress wearing a flannel top and blue jeans walked by carrying two pitchers of beer.

Tiffany pointed across the room. "Hey, aren't those the Walkers?"

Tracy followed her gaze and saw she was correct. Derrick and Abraham Walker were seated at a high top table next to the stage. They were deep in conversation, and Tracy tugged on Tiffany's arm.

"Don't point or stare," she cautioned her. "I don't want them to come over."

Isabella frowned. "Why not?" she asked. "That Derrick is a cutie."

"Stop being selfish," Tiffany spat. "You already flirted with the fishing guy. Save some cuties for the rest of us."

Isabella rolled her eyes.

"Let's grab some drinks," Tracy suggested. "I'll get the first round. What do you two want?"

"I'll take a Coors," Tiffany told her. "But here, take my credit card. You aren't paying for a single drink tonight."

Tracy obliged and put the card in her pocket. "Isabella?"

"A Tito's and soda with two ice cubes and three limes," she requested.

Tracy gave her a look. "I don't think they do cocktails here."

"Can you at least try?" Isabella asked impatiently. "That's the least you could do after making me change."

Tracy could not believe what was coming out of her friend's mouth, but she said nothing, instead walking away to fetch the drinks.

She returned moments later with a pitcher of beer and three mugs. Tracy furrowed her brow when she saw Derrick and Abraham were gathered around their table.

"You're back!" Isabella smiled at her. "But where is my drink?"

Tracy handed her a mug. "Here. They don't have cocktails."

Isabella turned up her nose. "I'll just get myself some water," she sniffed.

Tiffany nodded at Derrick and Abraham. "The Walkers came over to say hello," she explained as Derrick and Abraham tipped their baseball caps to greet her. "They recognized us from the farm."

"We felt bad for not formally introducing ourselves to our guests," Abraham smiled, staring at Isabella. "Especially when our guests are so beautiful."

Tiffany looked wistfully at Derrick, who was also staring at Isabella. "Are you both hanging out here for a while tonight? We just arrived, and this place is so cute."

Derrick responded, but kept his gaze on Isabella, who was enjoying the attention of both brothers. "We're about to take off," he sighed. "We are supposed to meet up with some friends at the sports bar by the interstate."

Isabella bit her lip. "That doesn't sound like any fun," she murmured, running her hands through her hair. "Why don't you stay here with us? I think we'll have a lot more fun *together*, don't you?"

Tracy wanted to vomit. Watching her friends preen and flirt was not her idea of an enjoyable evening.

"Let them go," she told Isabella. "They have plans, and we don't want to interfere."

"Please," Derrick said in a syrupy voice. "Please, interfere. The sports bar can wait, don't you think, Abraham?"

"I think it can," his brother agreed.

The Walker brothers pulled two stools up to the table and sat down. "How have you liked the farm and the town so far?" Abraham asked, his eyes sparkling as he looked at Isabella.

"It's different," she offered politely. "It's certainly different from the city."

"Hey, Derrick! Abraham!"

A young couple strode up to the table. "We're so sorry for your loss," the woman told them. "We heard the news about Charles."

"How is Holly holding up?" her husband inquired. "We know she and Charles were close."

The brothers exchanged looks before responding. "She's tough," Derrick said. "We'll make it through as a family."

"We'll be praying for you," the woman shared as she reached out and squeezed Abraham's shoulder. "The church has a basket to send over to the house, too."

"Thank you both so much," Derrick smiled softly. "Please tell your Mama we say hello, Martha."

"I will," the woman nodded.

"See y'all around," her husband waved goodbye.

As they left, two tall, leggy blonde women sauntered over. They appeared to be around Tracy's age.

"Boys," the woman on the left said. "How are you? We are so sorry about Charles."

"So sorry," her friend chimed in as she wrapped her arms around Derrick and then Abraham. "We can't believe it."

The men nodded. "Thank you," Abraham muttered.

"Our Mama is sending over a casserole for you tomorrow," the woman on the right smiled. "We hope you enjoy it."

They bid farewell and turned away, but not before Abraham blatantly checked out both girls.

Isabella narrowed her eyes at the Walker brothers. "Do you two know everyone in town?" she asked. It was clear she was annoyed they had been approached by the attractive women.

"It's a small town," Derrick described. "We know everyone."

The singer began belting out a lively song and Tiffany elbowed Tracy. "Look!" she exclaimed, pointing at the dance floor in front of the stage. "Those people are all doing the same dance moves at the same time."

Derrick jerked his head to look at Tiffany. "What? Y'all haven't seen line dancing before?"

Isabella giggled. "Only in the movies."

He reached for her hand and took it. "Let's go try it. You'll have fun."

Her face broke out into a grin as he led her away from the table and over to the dance floor.

Abraham looked over at Tiffany. "Care to join me?"

She nodded enthusiastically, and seconds later, Tracy was sitting alone at the table.

"Some bachelorette party this is," she groaned before taking a swig of her beer.

"Hey," an unfamiliar man's voice greeted her from behind. She turned to see one of the police officers who had been at the farm on the day of Charles' death.

"Oh, hi," she said in an unfriendly tone, remembering his impatience and gruff manner.

"Marty," he introduced himself. "I was one of the officers at the Walker farm."

"I remember you," she told him. "What are you doing here?"

He was dressed in jeans and a white button-down shirt. "I'm off duty," he smiled. "I am just enjoying a night off."

"Have a nice time," she replied dismissively before taking another drink of her beer.

"Tracy," he began, putting a hand on her table. "We need to talk."

"I thought this was your night off?"

He shook his head, the smile vanishing from his lips. "It's important. Can you please come outside with me?"

Tracy had a sinking feeling. Was this off duty officer up to something? Why did he need to talk with her?

"Come on," he urged her. "It'll only take a minute. Besides, I'm an officer of the law. If you don't come with me, I'll just have you arrested."

10

Tracy's mouth fell open in shock. Marty held up his hands. "That was a joke," he laughed innocently as he registered the look of fear on her face. "I'm sorry. That was mean."

"I'll say," she affirmed. "Seriously, do you need anything, or can I just get back to drinking my beer in peace?"

Marty looked into her eyes. "I do need to talk with you," he repeated. "But you don't need to worry. Come on, Tracy. I'm sorry about that joke. Just step outside with me and you'll be back to your beer before you know it."

Against her better judgment, Tracy followed him outside into the cool evening air.

"What do you want?" she asked, crossing her arms over her chest.

"Are you enjoying your time in town?" he asked, leaning casually against the wall of the building.

"I mean, I guess?" she replied, her voice filled with sarcasm. "A murder, my friends ditching me, and an unexpected farm stay weren't exactly my hopes for my bachelorette party."

He leaned in closer to her. She could smell his thick, musky cologne.

"I'm sorry to hear that," he offered. "If you give this town a chance, I think it will grow on you. We have great people and a rich culture here. Our town loves its traditions, and I hope you will get to experience some of the good stuff around these parts."

"The good stuff?"

He smiled. "Line dancing is a big deal. You should try it when you go back inside. We also have an annual Strawberry Festival with more food and games than you can imagine. Last year, we had a top Tim McGraw cover singer come to sing at the festival, and it was like seeing the real deal."

"That sounds…. interesting," she said.

"So it's your bachelorette party?" he asked. "I just got married last year. The newlywed life is fun. These are some of the best years of your life."

She uncrossed her arms and tucked a loose tendril of hair back into her bun. "Congratulations," she told him. "I hope you and your wife have a long, happy life together."

He stared at her. "That's what I wanted to talk to you about," he said in a hushed tone.

"Your wife?"

"Having a long, happy life," he corrected her. "Look, I don't want to scare you, but you need to be careful."

Tracy felt her heart begin to pound. "Careful? This town seems really quiet and safe."

"I don't mean in town," he shook his head. "I mean at the farm. With the Walkers."

Tracy studied his face. "What's wrong with the Walkers?" she asked him.

"They all hate each other," Marty elaborated, putting his hands on his waist. "They act like they are one big happy family, but they hate each other. Everyone in town knows it. Their parents weren't good people, and those Walkers have grown up to be hateful, spiteful people."

Tracy felt her stomach churn. "What are you trying to tell me?" she asked, hoping Marty would get to the point. "Do you think one of the Walkers *killed* Charles? Their own brother?"

Marty's face was grim. "I can't say," he whispered. "But I think you and your friends should be careful. It would be a shame if anything happened to you."

Before Tracy could reply, his phone began to ring. "The wife," he said as he looked at the screen. "I need to take this. Just remember, Tracy: keep your eyes open."

He walked away, leaving her alone outside of the bar.

Tracy felt nauseated as she weighed his words. Were they in danger at the farm? She felt her chest tighten as she walked back inside in search of her friends.

Isabella and Tiffany were on the dance floor with Abraham and Derrick. They were kicking and stepping in time with the music, and the two men were laughing as Isabella gave a playful twirl.

"Hey," she said in a hushed tone as she grabbed Tiffany's elbow. "I want to go home."

"What?" Tiffany shouted over the loud music. "I can't hear you."

"I want to go home," she repeated before turning to Isabella and tapping on her back. "Isabella? I want to go home."

The women stopped dancing and stared at Tracy. "Home? Already?" Isabella complained. "Tracy, come on. We are having fun."

Tracy looked at the Walker brothers. They were looking at her, and she had a pit in her stomach as she recalled Marty's warning.

"I'm tired," she lied. "It's *my* party. Let's go home."

Tiffany and Isabella complained as they said their goodbyes to the Walkers and trudged out of the bar. "We were having fun," Tiffany whined as Isabella unlocked the car.

"Tracy is a boring old married lady now," Isabella declared as she climbed into the driver's seat. "A buzzkill."

Tracy turned to look at her. "Why would you say something like that?" she asked. "It's my bachelorette party, and I am tired. Why can't you respect me and go with the flow?"

Isabella said nothing, turning to stare out the window as she navigated her way home.

As they pulled into the driveway, Tracy wrinkled her nose as she got a whiff of smoke.

"I wonder if Holly is having a bonfire," Tiffany wondered aloud as she rolled down her window.

They drew closer to the house. Tracy gasped as she realized where the smell was coming from.

The guest house was ablaze. Flames spilled out of the upstairs windows and dancing across the roof.

"Rose!" Tracy shrieked as she hastily parked the car and dashed outside. She sprinted toward the house, pumping her arms as she went. "Aunt Rose!"

The tinny wail of sirens filled the air. As Tracy ran toward the house, she felt her lungs aching; she enjoyed an occasional long-distance jog, but this pace was faster than any she had ever tried before.

"Aunt Rose!" she called out as she heard footsteps behind her.

Tiffany ran alongside Tracy. "Rose! Rose!"

They finally reached the front porch. Tracy collapsed onto the ground as the orange and red flames licked the left and center pillars of the porch. There was no way anyone could exit the house through the front door, and it looked like the roof might collapse. Tracy was unsure if her aunt was trapped in the building and hurt. She couldn't imagine life without her aunt.

"Aunt Rose!" she screamed as she fell to the floor.

11

"Tracy, get up," Tiffany urged her, bending down and trying to drag Tracy to her feet. "We have to go in there."

The sound of sirens grew closer. Tracy could not move.

"Is she inside?" Isabella asked as she finally caught up to them. She held her high heels in her hands.

"We don't know," Tiffany yelled as a firetruck pulled into the driveway. "Tracy? Can you see inside?"

Tracy could hardly bring herself to look at the burning house.

"Girls!"

The three women turned to see Rose running toward them. She was wearing her nightgown and had a quilt wrapped around her shoulders. Holly was right behind her.

Tracy stumbled as she tried to stand. She threw herself into her aunt's arms. "Are you okay?" she sobbed, unable to stop crying as she pressed herself into Rose's chest. "What happened? How did you get out?"

"Holly popped by and invited me to have tea with her at the main house," Rose explained. "We smelled smoke and called the fire department, and by the time we saw you girls pulling in, the guest house was on fire."

"I don't know what happened," Holly lamented as she shook her head. "I am so sorry, ladies."

Six firefighters emerged from the truck as it approached the house. Three men ran into the house, two women began shooting water from a large hose, and one man hurried over to talk with Holly.

"Ms. Walker? What's going on here?" he asked. "Is the fire contained to this building?"

"Yes," she nodded. "Thanks for coming out, Bill. I don't know how it started, but I am so glad my guests were not inside."

Bill looked at the women. "You're that bachelorette party that's in town, right?"

"How did you know that?" Tiffany asked in amazement.

"Small town," he replied in a gruff voice. "We'll do everything we can to save the house, Holly. I called for backup, so another truck will be here soon."

She smiled weakly. "Thank you so much."

"It's the least I can do," he shrugged. "With Charles dropping dead, this is the last thing your family needs to be worrying about. Now you ladies step back and let us get to work. Please move to a safe distance, at least a quarter mile away from the burning."

The women obeyed, moving back through the tall grass and eventually climbing into the car to wait out the fire. After nearly two hours, Bill returned, knocking on the driver's window.

Holly opened the car door. "What's the verdict?" she asked worriedly. "Are we gonna have to demolish it, Bill?"

He shook his head. "It's not as bad as we thought," he explained, and Tracy saw a look of relief flash across Holly's face. "Apart from a new roof, the repairs will be cosmetic. You got really lucky, Holly. This could have been so much worse."

Holly clapped a hand to her heart and held it there. "Oh, thank you, thank you," she said to Bill. "I am so grateful. That guest house has been in our family for generations, and I cannot believe we nearly lost it tonight."

Isabella blinked at the firefighter. "When will we be able to get in and go to bed?" she asked, stretching in a catlike fashion from where she sat in the backseat. "I am exhausted and need my beauty sleep."

He raised an eyebrow. "You won't."

"I won't what?" Isabella replied.

"You won't be going back inside tonight," he told them. "There was some severe smoke damage, and all the belongings and furniture inside of the house will have to be thrown out."

Tracy frowned, thinking of her cute luggage set and outfits that were likely gone forever. She was relieved to have worn her nice jewelry out to the bar, and she gingerly fingered her engagement ring.

"Our personal belongings will be thrown out?" Isabella screeched. "My makeup? My clothes? My curling iron? My haircare products?"

"We have plenty of clothes and toiletries at the house," Holly offered graciously, but Isabella ignored her.

"My things are worth thousands of dollars. This cannot be happening. How will I make it without my keratin hair cream? Or my personalized skincare regimen? Or my Prada bag?"

"I thought you had your Prada bag with you tonight?" Tiffany added.

"This is my *GUCCI* bag," Isabella rolled her eyes. "The Prada bag is *much* nicer."

The firefighter looked at Holly. "We'll get out of here and let you all rest," he told her. "

I'll give you a call tomorrow and have my guys check into this fire."

"Thank you," Holly sighed. "Thank you so much."

As he walked away, Holly closed her eyes and took several long, deep breaths. Tracy counted ten inhales and eleven exhales. When she was through, she opened her eyes and looked at the women.

"I'm sure you are all so tired," she said softly. "Come on-we have plenty of room at the main house. We have clothes, shampoo and blankets. You can stay with us and then leave first thing in the morning."

"Leave?" Isabella asked. "I'm not leaving this place without my Prada bag. Surely someone can go into the house and fetch it for me. I'll ask Derrick to do it for me."

"Whatever you want," Holly replied, the defeat evident in her voice. "But for now, let's go to the house and get to sleep. It's been a long night for all of us and I am *dying* to be in my bed."

12

After a few hours of fitful sleep, Tracy felt enraged when the cry of a rooster woke her up before dawn. She checked her watch and realized it was five in the morning.

She rolled over, her back touching Tiffany's in the queen-sized bed they were sharing at the main house. Tiffany was snoring loudly, and Tracy could hardly contain her annoyance.

"Tiffany," she whispered loudly. "You're snoring."

The young woman opened one eye. "What? Sorry. So sorry."

Tiffany turned over and went right back to sleep. It was finally quiet, and Tracy closed her eyes and settled down.

Seconds later, Tiffany began to snore again. Tracy moaned. After thirty minutes of tossing and turning, she finally rose from the bed, dressing in the soft flannel shirt and jeans Holly had given her the night before.

She tiptoed downstairs, hoping she could catch a few more minutes of sleep on the plaid couch in the living room. Tracy did not want to risk running into Derrick or Abraham, but Holly had shared that the two regularly crashed with friends in town, and they had not been home when the ladies had trooped in the night before.

She was dismayed to find Holly sitting at the kitchen table reading a newspaper when she arrived on the first floor.

"You're up early," she commented as Holly looked up at her.

"You know what they say," Holly replied cheerfully. "The early bird gets the worm!"

Tracy shuddered as she remembered the pale, slimy worms from their fishing expedition.

"Can I make some breakfast for you?" Holly asked. "Eggs? Bacon? Muffins?"

Tracy shook her head. "I'm fine," politely declined. "Do you have a busy day ahead of you?"

"Not really," Holly shared. "But *you* do!"

Tracy was puzzled. "What do you mean?"

Holly placed the newspaper down on the table and beckoned at the chair beside her. "Please, sit down."

Tracy obliged.

"I feel so terrible about the weekend you've had," Holly apologized. Tracy noticed the dark circles beneath her eyes.

"It isn't your fault," Tracy assured her.

"But I want you to have the best time," Holly told her. "I know a lot has happened, but I want to make it up to you."

"You do not have to make anything up to me," Tracy insisted, but Holly went on.

"I stayed up all night looking into activities for y'all," Holly told her, her eyes twinkling with excitement. "And I scheduled an appointment for you today at a day spa!"

"There is a day spa here?" Tracy asked incredulously. "In this town?"

"Well, it's more of a local beauty parlor," Holly admitted sheepishly. "But they do manicures and pedicures and some waxing treatments. I've booked and prepaid for an appointment for the group to go this morning. What do you think?"

Tracy was touched by the gesture. "You really didn't have to do that," she said to Holly. "You've been through so much. You deserve the pampering. Please tell me you are coming with us?"

"I have to stay and meet with the fire chief," Holly explained. "But maybe I could join you all for dinner tonight?"

"We would love that," Tracy smiled. "Thank you so much."

Holly clapped her hands together. "Thank *you* for being so sweet despite all the hiccups this weekend," she praised Tracy. "Now, why don't you go wake the girls? I'll get breakfast started and you all can eat and then enjoy your day."

Breakfast was served thirty minutes later, and Tracy was in awe of the spread Holly had put together for them. The table was filled with plates of warm toast, three kinds of homemade jam, fresh fruit, thick bacon, hard-boiled eggs, cinnamon rolls, freshly squeezed juices, and porridge, and Tracy licked her lips at the sight and smell of it all.

"You've done too much," Rose insisted as she entered the kitchen. She was dressed in a pair of men's cotton pajamas, and she was practically swimming in them as she tried to roll up the sleeves.

"This looks amazing," Tiffany exclaimed, taking a seat at the table. "Holly, you are so nice to do all of this for us."

Tracy watched as Isabella glanced at each plate. "I can eat the fruit," she muttered to herself.

Holly leaned her head forward. "Sorry, what was that? I didn't hear you, Isabella. Will this breakfast work for you?"

Isabella gave a condescending smirk. "It looks nice if you are into carbs and fats," she began. "But I try to eat clean. Do you have any yogurt?"

Holly was unphased. "Sure! Be right back."

She returned a moment later with a long pink tube the size of a ruler. "Here."

Isabella held it between her thumb and pointer finger as if it were a dead fish. "What is this?"

"It's yogurt," Holly smiled. "Abraham likes to freeze these tubes and eat them on hot days."

Isabella examined the packaging. "It has artificial flavors and contains fat."

She wrinkled her nose. "I don't want to risk upsetting my stomach. I'll just have some fruit."

Isabella tossed the tube of yogurt into the trash can beside the sink.

"Wait!" Holly stopped her. "That was unused. We don't want to waste it."

She bent over and fished the yogurt out of the trashcan. "See? It's just fine for someone else. I'll put it back into the refrigerator. Now, ladies, sit! Eat! Enjoy."

They sat down as Holly turned to open the refrigerator. Tracy glowered at Isabella. "Be nice," she mouthed, hoping her friend would get the message.

"Holly," Rose said as she joined them at the table. "Tracy told us about the lovely day you planned for us. It was so sweet of you to make the reservation, but I am just so tired from last night. I would prefer to stay back and relax. Is it possible for you to call the beauty parlor and let them know?"

"Wait," Tracy jerked her head toward her aunt. "You don't want to come?"

"Rose," Tiffany pleaded. "Please come. It'll be good for you. And besides, it's Tracy's party. If she wants you to come, you have to come!"

Rose took a deep breath. "Okay, okay," she relented. "I can just take a nap later today. I'll come."

Tiffany grinned, showing both rows of her teeth. "YAY!"

While the beginning of Tracy's bachelorette weekend had been a disaster, the salon day Holly had planned for them was a hit. Regina, the owner of the beauty parlor, was hospitable and funny; she and her two staff members catered to the women's every request.

The three-hour visit began with manicures and pedicures for each woman. Tracy chose a bright white polish for her fingers and toes, and the nail technician even added tiny rhinestones to her ring finger in celebration of her upcoming nuptials.

"You should come back here for your wedding day nails," Rose cheered up seeing the manicure. "Your hands look like a model's!"

After their hands were massaged, the pedicures began. Despite the salon being out of the color Isabella had selected, she was courteous to the staff and did not make a big deal out of the incident. Everyone had a blast, and while they were waiting for their nails to dry, Regina served them special plum mimosas.

"We used local plums that are in season, so these will be delicious. Cheers!" she said as she handed Tracy her flute.

Tracy leaned back in her lounge chair. She finally felt relaxed.

"This is what a bachelorette weekend should feel like," she thought to herself, closing her eyes briefly.

A soft tap on her knee brought her back to reality.

"So sorry to bother you," Jackie Belle, Regina's assistant apologized. "But we have one last bit of pampering for the bride-to-be. Would you be interested in a brief scalp massage? We had a cancellation this morning and had some extra time, and we wanted to offer it to the bride."

Tracy's face lit up. "Absolutely," she told Jackie Belle as the others smiled at her.

"Wonderful," the assistant nodded. "I'll come around back and get started. Just close your eyes and take some deep breaths. It'll feel amazing."

She moved to stand behind Tracy's lounge chair. Tracy let her head droop over the back of the beige leather chair, and Jackie Belle carefully began to wind her fingers through

Tracy's hair. Tracy relaxed her shoulders, trying to tune out the chattering of her friends as they talked to each other.

"So I hear you are from out of town?" Jackie Belle asked softly as she wove her fingers through Tracy's scalp.

"Yes, a few hours away from here," she answered, enjoying the sensation of Jackie Belle rubbing her fingertips across her forehead.

"Where are you girls staying?"

"We were staying at the Walkers' guest house, but now, we are staying in their main house. It's a long story."

Jackie Belle stopped moving her hands. "You're staying at the Walkers?" she asked, her voice shaking. "In their home?"

"Yes?" she replied, wondering what the issue was. "Didn't Holly tell you when she made the appointment?"

Jackie Belle squeezed Tracy's head harder than she had before.

"The pressure is too much," she squeaked. "Can you please ease off?"

Jackie Belle let go. "I'm sorry," she fretted as Tracy sat up and turned around to look at her. "I was just shocked."

"Shocked?"

She nodded. "Holly Walker is a nice enough gal, but everyone in town knows that the Walker family and that house of theirs is *cursed*."

13

Tracy's head was spinning as Jackie Belle made her shocking declaration about the Walker family. She looked at her friends. Their stunned faces made it clear that they had also heard what Jackie Belle had said.

"What do you mean? Cursed?" Tracy asked as she furrowed her brow.

"It's just as I said," Jackie Belle whispered.

Everyone leaned in closer to hear her.

"That family has had more bad luck than any family this town has ever seen. Bad things always seem to happen to the Walkers, and more often than not, those bad things take place at their farm."

Isabella's mouth fell open. "The fire!" she screeched as Jackie Belle stared at her. "There was a fire on the property last night. Our things were damaged and the guest house nearly burned down."

"See?" Jackie Belle nodded. "That's exactly the kind of thing I am talking about."

Tracy peered at her aunt. "Aunt Rose? What do you think about all of this?"

Rose bit her lip. "I'm a practical person," she informed the group. "And I don't have a lot of patience for tomfoolery. I'm not sure if I believe in this curse business."

Jackie Belle reached out and touched Rose's arm. "Ma'am, it isn't tomfoolery," she protested. "Bad things happen there. The Walker parents?"

"The ones who died and left the siblings to raise themselves?" Tracy followed up.

"Exactly. You have a good memory," Jackie Belle told her. "Well, it all begins with that lie they tell about their people coming to town on the Oregon Trail. Everyone in town knows it's untrue. The old librarian at the historical society did some digging into the Walker family, and the truth is that they came and took this land from a Native American tribe. I think it was a family of Klamath people. The Walkers came to town and ran the Native Americans off of the land. When they returned to fight back, the Walkers killed them all. They murdered the women and children, too."

Tiffany's face paled. "Is that true?"

Jackie Belle put her hands on her hips. "The records are public! It's all true. The first Walkers to come to this town were bad folks, and that bad blood has made its way down to the very Walkers whose home you are staying in right now."

Isabella stood up. She looked tired and older than her age, without her usual array of makeup. She was dressed in a borrowed pair of black leggings and an oversized Oregon

State t-shirt, but she still held herself with her usual air of authority.

"This is nonsense," Isabella announced. "This is rude and tacky. *Everyone* probably had ancestors who did bad things. In fact, I know some of my ancestors on the east coast had indentured servants. That was not a kind practice."

Rose agreed. "Everyone has unfavorable roots," she told the group. "Somewhere in every single person's lineage, there was someone, or a group of people, who did awful things. That doesn't mean we should hold those mistakes against people who had nothing to do with the crimes of their ancestors. That would be a terrible misstep."

Jackie Belle narrowed her eyes at Rose and Isabella. "You don't believe me," she murmured as she wiped her hands on the blue smock covering her clothing. "You don't believe that the Walkers are cursed."

Tracy wanted to know more. "I am curious about the curse," she told Jackie Belle. "Who put the curse on them? Were they already cursed when they showed up here?"

Tiffany bobbed her head. "I want to know, too."

"Legend says that a Native American Chief cursed the family and the land after his family was killed on the Walker land," she shared. "Until the Walkers atone for what their people did, they will never live happy, long lives. No Walker who has stayed here in town has lived past the age of fifty, and no Walker ever will."

Tiffany blinked. "Could the curse hurt us?"

Jackie Belle nodded emphatically. "Yes. It does not discriminate. Ask Holly about her childhood friend, Tonya. The little girl mysteriously had a seizure and died at the

Walker house. They were two years older than me in school, and I still remember having to go to Tonya's funeral. Or the cousins of theirs that came to stay for the summer? The entire lot of them drowned in the river behind the property. It's the curse."

Tracy felt anxious, and she saw that the others looked nervous as well. "What should we do?" she wondered aloud as her friends stared at her.

"Run," Jackie Belle urged her. "You all should call a cab and leave from here. It isn't safe there."

Isabella scoffed. "I'm not leaving this town until the firefighters dig out our things and I get my Prada bag back," she insisted. "These stories are unbecoming, Tracy. We really shouldn't be investing energy into these lies."

"They aren't lies," Jackie Belle promised.

Rose nodded. "I think Isabella is right," she added. "I think we need to take all of this with a grain of salt. It all sounds like the Walkers have had some horrible tragedies, and we shouldn't be making light of their traumas."

Tiffany glanced at Tracy. "Tracy? What do you think? Should we go home or go back to the farm?"

"I can call a cab right now," Jackie Belle offered. "I can help get you out of here."

Everyone looked at Tracy. "What do you want to do?" Rose asked her quietly. "What do you want to do next, dear?"

14

Before Tracy could reply, the front door of the beauty parlor opened. A tall woman with thick brunette hair across her shoulders strode in. She appeared to be in her early forties. She was very beautiful, with green eyes and a few freckles across her rosy cheeks.

"You must be the bachelorette party! I'm Molly. Molly Walker."

At the mention of the Walker surname, Jackie Belle turned on her heel and scurried away to the back room.

"What's her deal?" Molly asked with a laugh. "Did I scare her off?"

"You have no idea," Tiffany muttered before Tracy jabbed her in the side with her elbow.

"My sister told me all about you girls," Molly shared as she sat down in the chair next to Tracy's. "I live out of town, but I came as soon as I heard the news. Holly said you gals were down here having a spa day, and I thought I could pop by and say hello before I run some errands."

"Molly, it is so nice to meet you. We are *so* sorry for your loss," Rose told her.

"Oh, don't worry about it! The guesthouse will be put back together in a few weeks, no? Holly said that the interior looks rough, but the contractors she called promised they would start the repairs next week."

Tracy stared at the elder Walker sister. "We're sorry for the loss of your *brother*," she clarified as Molly's eyes widened.

"Oh. Thank you," she said briskly. "That's very kind of you."

Rose studied Molly's face. "Were you two close?"

Molly shrugged. "Besides my sister, I'm not really close with any other members of my family. I left town as soon as I could," she described. "I hated leaving Holly behind, but I wanted to go to college in New York City. She was too little to come with me, and I had to do what was best for myself at the time."

Tracy saw Isabella checking out Molly's outfit. She was wearing a pair of tailored trousers with a casual pink blazer and white sneakers. Her hoop earrings sparkled in the light of the salon, and a large, glittering wedding ring sparkled on her left hand.

"New York, huh?" Isabella asked. "You definitely don't look like you're from around here."

Molly chuckled. "You should have seen me in high school," she told them. "Before I moved away, I wore my flannels and jeans and boots like everyone else around here. I usually dress down when I come to town, but I came straight here from the airport and haven't had a chance to change."

Tracy smiled kindly at the newcomer. "Will you be in town for a while?"

Molly's expression darkened. "As long as I'm needed," she replied ominously. "Holly told me I didn't have to come back for the funeral, but my husband would think I was a monster if I didn't. The real monster is dead, though."

"Charles?" Tiffany asked.

"I shouldn't have said that. Forgive me. I probably am jet-lagged," Molly apologized as she stood up. "I need to go to the house and check on Holly, but it was nice meeting you all. Holly said we all will be having dinner together tonight, and I am so looking forward to it."

Tracy stared at her as she left the salon. "That was odd," she said aloud as her phone began to ring. She hoped it was her fiance and was disappointed when she realized it was Holly.

"Hey," she greeted their hostess. "Guess who we just met? Your sister, Molly, came to the salon."

"That's great. She was so excited to meet all of you," Holly informed her. "Hey, I have some incredible news. A contractor in town owed me a favor, and they were able to speed up some of the construction work. The master suite is a bit of a mess and needs more work, but you gals can get back into the guesthouse, if you'd like. I had a cleaning crew come out, too. It stinks a bit, but if you leave the windows and doors open, it should be good as new."

"Really? That's great news. Were they able to salvage any of our things?"

"Most of them," Holly said. "There were a few pieces of clothing that had smoke damage, but other than that, the toiletries and electronics came out okay."

"Wow," Tracy exclaimed. "I'll tell the girls. Thanks for letting me know."

She ended the call and shared the good news with her friends.

"And my purse?" Isabella asked hopefully. "Did they save it?"

"...Holly didn't say," Tracy sighed. "But our makeup and electronics are okay, and if we want, we can stay there tonight instead of the main house."

Rose grinned. "I pride myself on being an easy-going lady, but I am sure excited to have my hair cream and nail clippers back!"

Tiffany giggled. "And I can't wait to have my hair scrunchies back. The rubber bands Holly gave me to use for a ponytail are so rough."

"Well, shall we go?" Isabella asked. "Reunite with our things?"

Tracy nodded. "Let's get out of here."

When they arrived at the guesthouse, they saw a police car parked outside.

"Oh no," Isabella grumbled as Rose parked the car. "Not this again."

Tracy saw Marty standing on the porch. He was dressed in his uniform, and he had a grim look on his face.

"Hey," she greeted him as she approached the guest house. "What's going on? I thought this place was cleared?"

He stared at her. "Where have you four been all day?"

Tiffany smiled. "The salon," she explained. "We had a little spa day, thanks to Holly."

Marty took a pad of paper out of his pocket and scribbled a note.

"What's that for?" Rose asked. "Is everything okay?"

The officer tucked his notepad back into his pocket and put his hands on his waist. "We'll be coming back through with a team to search the property," he informed the ladies. "It seems Charles Walker's death is a bit more… suspect… than we first believed."

Tracy's nostrils flared. "What? His death? What are you talking about?"

Marty stared into her eyes. "My team and I have every reason to believe that Charles Walker was murdered," he stated in a business-like tone. "And someone on this property has tampered with evidence."

"Tampered with evidence?" Isabella asked. "How? Who?"

"We don't know… *yet*," Marty told them. "But we will find out. Someone on this farm knows something, and I won't rest until I find out what happened to Charles Walker."

15

As Marty pulled away in his squad car, the women stood silently on the porch of the guesthouse. Finally, Isabella spoke. "We should just go in," she suggested, reaching for the doorknob. "I need to see if my bag is in there."

"Enough about your Prada bag," Tracy huffed. "There are bigger things going on than you having a reunion with your *purse*, Isabella."

Her friend's jaw dropped. "I can't believe you just said that to me," she frowned.

"She isn't wrong," Tiffany chimed in.

Rose sighed. "Enough of this, ladies," she urged them. "Let's just get inside and get our bearings."

They were all pleasantly surprised to find that while the inside of the guesthouse was a bit dusty and smelled of smoke, the furniture and decor was intact.

"This isn't so bad," Rose smiled as she surveyed the front room. "Holly must be so relieved!"

Isabella raced upstairs. She was silent. Moments later, she stormed downstairs and stomped over to a couch, and sat down. "It isn't there," she grumbled, crossing her arms.

"Let's chat about last night," Tracy suggested, ignoring her pouting friend. "We don't want the police to think we are mixed up in all of this. Aunt Rose, do you remember anything? You were here longer than we were yesterday..."

Rose took a seat on the couch next to Isabella.

"Well," she began, folding her hands together and closing her eyes. "Something strange did happen before I went over to Holly's last night..."

Tiffany's eyes widened. "What happened?!"

Rose looked over at the staircase. "I was sitting on the couch reading, and out of the blue, I started hearing things upstairs."

"Hearing things?" Tracy pressed her. "What kinds of things?"

Rose exhaled. "It sounded like someone was walking around up there," she explained. "You girls were gone, and I knew no one was up there, but it spooked me. I nearly jumped out of my skin when Holly knocked on the door and asked if I wanted to have tea with her."

Tracy stared at her aunt. "Did you tell Holly about what you heard?"

Rose shook her head. "No, I was a little embarrassed," she admitted. "I didn't want her to think I was paranoid or a silly old woman or something."

Tracy moved to sit next to her aunt. "You aren't a silly old woman," she promised her. "Did you hear or see anything else?"

Rose thought for a moment. "I heard some banging noises outside," she shared. "When I peeked outside, it looked like those Walker brothers were out there being rowdy. It looked like the pair of them were roughhousing in the field by the main house. I thought they were just silly boys being boys."

"Derrick and Abraham?" Tiffany asked.

"What time did you see them?" Tracy asked. "We ran into them at the bar last night… they couldn't have been here."

Rose pursed her lips. "Maybe nine or ten?"

"They were with us then," Isabella insisted primly. "They couldn't have been here. You must be mistaken."

Rose raised an eyebrow. "Then who was outside?"

No one spoke. The silence was awkward, and Tracy felt the tension in the room.

"I'm going to take a nap," Isabella declared after a few moments. "Can I borrow someone's toothpaste? My toiletry bag *and* purse seem to have vanished in the chaos… we also need toilet paper, too."

Tracy stood up. "I'll pop over to the main house," she offered, eager to take a break from the group. "Be back soon."

She exited the guesthouse and started walking toward the main house. She wondered who and what her aunt had seen and heard the night before. Was someone else running around on the property? Had someone been inside of the guesthouse before the fire?

Lost in thought, Tracy walked right into Derrick Walker, who was bent over tying his shoe on the front step of the main house.

"Sorry," she apologized as he stared up at her.

"You lost?" he asked. "Where's your friend? I had fun chatting with Ismay last night. She's gorgeous."

"Isabella," she corrected him. "Hey, speaking of last night, what did you guys do after we left?"

"We… I… I went home right after," he answered quickly.

Tracy studied his face for any signs of deceit and noticed he was clenching his jaw tightly.

"And before the country bar?"

"Why are you asking?" he questioned her, rising to his feet and drawing himself to his full height. "Is it really your business? Why do you care so much about what I was up to yesterday?"

"Ummm, no reason," she replied, trying to sound confident and cool. "I was just curious. We don't know a lot about the area, so I am trying to make some plans for us while we are in town."

"Really?" he asked.

"Really," she confirmed.

He stared at her, and the intensity of his green-eyed gaze sent a shiver down her back. She felt as though he could see right into her soul, and in that moment, she wanted nothing more than to turn on her heel and run away from Derrick and the Walker farm forever.

16

Derrick's face broke into a smile. "Well, if you and *Isabella* need some recommendations for some fun around here, you just ask. I'm happy to help."

She exhaled deeply, feeling relief wash over her. "Thanks."

He looked at her inquisitively. "What brought you over here today? Did you need something from the main house?"

Tracy nodded. "We're out of toilet paper," she shared. "Can I get some from the house?"

"Sure thing," he agreed, moving to open the front door for her. "I'll take you down to the basement and you can grab as many rolls as you'd like."

The basement was dark and eerie, with wet concrete walls, damp air, and no windows.

"It ain't pretty down here, but we have a ton of storage space," he informed her as he gestured at a wall of metal lockers across from the stairwell. "This is where we keep the supplies for the house, so if you ever need anything, feel free to wander back down."

"I think I'm too much of a scaredy-cat to come down here alone," she laughed, hoping self-deprecation would help her win some points with Derrick. He made her feel uneasy, and she hoped following him down into the grim, dusty basement was not a mistake.

He unlocked the second locker from the right and scowled. "No toilet paper," he groaned. "I told Holly to get some last week. Sorry."

Derrick led her back upstairs. "I can run into town and grab some for you girls," he suggested. "It won't take long."

Tracy peeked out the kitchen window. It was a sunny, warm day, and she was aching to be outside.

"I'll go," she told him as she started to move toward the door. "It's a nice day. I'll walk into town, get some fresh air, and be back by dinner time."

"Are you sure?" Derrick asked. "It's no trouble for me to get it for you."

Tracy nodded. "I want to get my steps in," she insisted.

"I don't know what that means, but I hope you enjoy it," he waved as she turned and left the main house.

Tracy set off toward town with an extra bounce in her step; she was grateful for some time alone, and she was looking forward to some time to process the events of the weekend. So much had happened in a few short days, and as she walked, she reflected on her time away from home.

She pulled her phone out of her pocket and stared at it, willing it to ring. Warren had texted her while she was getting her pedicure, but the message was short and impersonal:

Hey, babe! Having a blast here. Vegas is crazy. Hope you are having a good time with the girls. XO

She stuffed the phone back into her pocket. She wished her fiance had at least *called* her. She had sent him several photos, texts, and had even left a sweet voicemail for him. Why wasn't he communicating with *her*? Had something happened to him? His groomsmen had been posting about the weekend all over their social media accounts, so she knew everything must be fine.

Still, she knew that Las Vegas was a hotbed for bad behavior, and even though she loved and trusted Warren, she worried that the city and nightlife being so "crazy" weren't good for him.

The sound of a car honking snapped her back to reality. A minivan buzzed past her, narrowly avoiding hitting Tracy. She rushed to the side of the road, thankful she hadn't been hurt.

When she arrived in town, she hurried to the grocery store. She was surprised that the sky was beginning to darken, and she worried it might rain.

"Excuse me," she stopped a store clerk at the cashier's stand. "I need some help. Can you tell me where the toilet paper is?"

The clerk smiled at her. She was a heavyset woman with deep set eyes and short curly blonde hair. "Aisle six, sweetie. Come back if you can't find it and I'll help you."

"Thanks," Tracy smiled.

She turned left and walked down aisle six. As she approached the shelves of toilet paper, paper towels, and cleaning supplies, she noticed a woman was staring at her from the end of the aisle.

Tracy brushed it off. She studied the shelves and chose a package of toilet paper that was big enough to last the group the rest of the trip, but small enough that she could manage to walk home with it.

As she turned to return to the checkout line, she saw the woman was still staring at her. She was beautiful; with long, thick black hair that fell to her waist, dark brown eyes, and a long, straight nose, she could have easily been a runway model or a movie star.

She gave a friendly little wave, which Tracy returned. She then squinted at Tracy, peering at her face with intense curiosity. Finally, the woman spoke.

"Tracy!" the woman called out. "Tracy, is that you?"

Tracy stopped in her tracks. "I'm Tracy," she confirmed as the woman drew closer to her.

"Well, what do we have here? I can't believe it. It's *you*. Tracy," the stranger smiled. "I've been *dying* to meet you, Tracy."

17

Tracy stared at the woman. "Do we know each other?" she asked slowly. "I've never been to the area before, but have we met?"

The woman laughed. "Oh, no, silly. I'm sorry, I probably frightened you."

She stuck out her hand. "I'm Monica, Monica Walker."

Tracy shook Monica's outstretched hand. "Monica *Walker*?"

Monica bobbed her head in agreement. "Yes, that's my name. I'm sure you've met a million and two Walkers over the last few days, huh? It's a big family."

"Are you a cousin?" Tracy asked, assuming that Monica was in town for the funeral. "How are you related to Holly and her family?"

Monica's smile disappeared. "Derrick didn't tell you? I'm his *wife*."

Tracy nodded enthusiastically. "Oh, silly me," she chided herself. "I am such an airhead. Of course, Derrick mentioned you, his gorgeous wife," she lied.

Her mind was spinning. Why hadn't Derrick mentioned he was married? He sure hadn't brought up his wife while he was flirting with Isabella last night, nor had he said anything to Tracy when she was at the house.

Monica's face brightened. "We've been married for ten years next summer," she shared. "Derrick is my soulmate."

"He's said great things about you," Tracy fibbed, hoping Monica couldn't see the panic she was feeling on the inside. Why hadn't Derrick mentioned he was *married*? What other secrets was he keeping?

"He's said such wonderful things about all of you," Monica gushed to Tracy. "That's how I knew it was you. Derrick described all of you to a T! You, your aunt, your younger friend, and the interesting one."

"The interesting one?"

Monica rolled her eyes. "Derrick says one of your guests is a little bit of a prima donna."

"Oh, did he say that?" Tracy asked. Derrick sure hadn't seemed bothered by Isabella's prim, high maintenance personality when he had been line dancing with her last night. "I'm glad he is glad we are there. The farm is so nice."

"It's a lovely property," Monica agreed. "There is so much to offer around here, too. The people are so nice, the town is safe, and the natural beauty is unmatched. Between the rolling hills and the woods, this place is America's best kept secret."

"I think *Monica is* another best kept secret," Tracy thought to herself as Monica chattered on.

"Derrick says you're settling in and enjoying our small town. He said you have a few things planned. I hope he and Abraham have been helpful?"

"They've been," Tracy nodded. "But we were so bummed you haven't been able to join us thus far. What were you up to last night?"

Monica shrugged. "You know, just a few things here and there."

"Oh? What do you like to do for fun?"

Monica bit her lip. "Well, last night, I went to the grocery, came home, and relaxed."

Tracy looked around. "Back at the grocery so soon?"

She could tell Monica was holding something back, and she wanted to get to the bottom of it.

"We ran out of a few things and Derrick asked me to make his favorite summer salad for supper," Monica replied.

Tracy sensed there was something Monica was hiding. "What time did he get home last night?"

"I don't know," the Walker wife answered. "Are you the police or something? I think he got in pretty late?"

Tracy thought for a moment. The women had arrived back at the burning guesthouse at 11:15. Had *Derrick* been there before them?

"Sorry, I'm just chatty," Tracy lied, hoping Monica wouldn't detect her suspicion.

"It must be a city girl thing," Monica commented. "My sister-in-law is from New York City, and man, she can talk the ears off of a piece of corn."

"Molly?"

"Have you two met?" Monica asked. "Molly is Derrick's favorite sibling. Oh, I shouldn't have said that. Siblings shouldn't have favorites."

Tracy laughed. "I won't tell," she promised. "Why is Molly his favorite?"

Monica shrugged. "My husband's parents died too young," she began. "They left the kids to raise themselves. Old Charlie was a big grouch, Abraham is sneaky as the devil and was always up to no good, Holly worshiped Charlie and only listened to him, and that left Derrick and Molly to fend for themselves. He was devastated when she went off to school in New York, but I know he's glad she's back now."

"Molly seems really interesting. How long is she staying in town?"

"Until Holly lights a fire under her own behind and gets the darn funeral planned for Charlie," Monica complained. "She is moving slow as molasses, and the rest of us are ready to move on. Charlie only looked out for himself, and even though Holly adored him, the rest of us know the truth."

Tracy stared at her. "The truth?"

"That he gambled away a huge portion of the family money, which is why Holly couldn't afford to go away to college, why we almost lost the farm, and why Abraham couldn't make the down payment for the house he was trying to buy a few years back. It was a disaster. Charlie got drunk and gambled away so much money that Molly had to send every one of her paychecks from her fancy job in New York back to the family for *two* years."

"Are you kidding?" Tracy asked, shocked by this information.

"I wish I were," Monica replied. "Look, I've probably gossiped enough about our family for one night. I need to get home and start grilling these steaks. Tracy, it was so nice to meet you!" Monica gave a cheerful wave as she walked away.

"And you," Tracy replied quietly, feeling a tightness in her chest that she had not been experiencing before her chance encounter with Mrs. Derrick Walker.

When Tracy arrived back at the guesthouse, she found her friends playing cards on the front porch.

"Then you have to take the last card," Isabella explained to Tiffany as Tracy climbed the steps. "Hey, you're back."

Tracy produced the toilet paper from the plastic sack and waved it at them. "Ta da. Where is Aunt Rose? Is she napping?"

Tiffany stuck her tongue out at Tracy. "Very funny, Tracy."

Tracy dropped the grocery bag. "Wait, what?"

Isabella gave her a puzzled look. "Rose is with you, isn't she?"

"No," Tracy replied, feeling a knot in her stomach. "I went to town by myself."

She tore into the house and went through every room. After a few minutes, Tracy realized her search was in vain. Her aunt was nowhere to be found.

18

"Did she leave a note?" Tiffany asked as Tracy raced down the stairs. "Or a text?"

"I don't know," Tracy worried as she threw open the door to the tiny closet under the stairs and peeked in. "I haven't gotten any calls or texts from her. Have either of you?"

Tiffany shook her head. "No," she frowned as she looked at Isabella.

"I haven't, either."

"I'm going to call her," Tracy decided, dialing Rose's number.

The familiar strains of "Don't Rain on My Parade", her ringtone, tinkled from upstairs.

"She *must* be asleep or something," Tracy sighed in relief. "Her phone is ringing upstairs."

Tracy hurried back upstairs and dashed into the bunkroom. She peeked down into Rose's bunk. It was empty, but Tracy saw a small rectangular object on the pillow. She bent down to examine it and realized it was her aunt's cell phone.

Tracy picked up the cell phone and peered at the screen. It was a photo of Rose and Tracy taken last summer during an evening out at a local winery. Tracy was making a silly face, and Rose was gazing at her niece with adoration.

"Where are you?" she muttered to herself as she tucked Rose's phone into her pocket.

When she returned downstairs, she found Tiffany using the house phone.

"Yes, Officer," Tiffany said before mouthing 'police' at Tracy. "No, I don't think she is under duress."

Tracy watched her, grateful Tiffany had the presence of mind to call the police. After being frightened the night before by her aunt's near brush with death during the fire, all Tracy wanted to do was find her and hug her.

"Absolutely," Tiffany continued, her lips turned downward into a frown. "I understand. Thanks."

She hung up the phone and stared at Tracy. "The police say it's too soon to file a missing person report. They said we have to wait at least twenty-four hours before she is officially considered to be missing."

"Seriously?" Tracy huffed. "That's ridiculous. Her phone is here, her purse is upstairs, and no one has any missed calls or text messages from her."

Isabella stopped her. "Wait," she urged. "Take a breath. What if we are blowing things out of proportion? Maybe she just took a walk into town or something?"

"I would have seen her if she had gone to town," Tracy protested, feeling a sharp ache in her head. "And she would have left a note or called or something."

Isabella nodded. "Okay, okay," she agreed. "Slow down. Take some breaths. You are shaking, Tracy, and that can't be good for you."

Tracy sank down on the couch. "Let's go talk to Holly," she suggested. "Maybe Rose is just up at the main house. Maybe I *am* blowing things out of proportion."

Tiffany took her hand and gave it a squeeze. "We'll find her. I promise."

The three women hurried over to the main house and knocked on the door. Holly answered it, smiling as she welcomed the ladies inside.

"What are y'all up to?" she asked as they spilled into the kitchen. "Do you want a snack?"

"Have you seen my aunt?" Tracy asked, her voice tinged with fear. "We can't find her anywhere, and no one has heard from her."

Holly's eyes widened. "She isn't here," she revealed as she rolled up the sleeves of her red and pink button-down shirt. "I haven't heard from her, either."

Tracy's mouth went dry. "Oh, my goodness…"

Holly held out her hands with her palms facing Tracy. "Stop," she cautioned her. "Take a deep breath. This is a safe town. Maybe Rose went for a long walk to rest and reset. Last night, she and I were talking about the natural beauty around these parts. Perhaps she is down by the river at the edge of the property…"

Tracy's heart beat rapidly in her chest as she remembered Jackie Belle's warning at the salon. She recalled the story of the Walker cousins who had drowned at the river, and it made her sick to her stomach.

"She left her cell phone at the guesthouse," Tracy said, reaching into her pocket and pulling out the phone. "She never leaves her phone behind."

Holly took her by the shoulders and stared into her face. "Hey," she began in a soft voice. "Tracy, relax. Everything is going to be okay. I'm sure Rose is just out enjoying some nature or in town. It's not even dark outside yet. I wouldn't worry."

Isabella nodded. "She's right, Tracy," she added, tucking a loose strand of hair behind her ear. "We need to calm down. There is no reason to believe she is unsafe or in trouble. She's probably out shopping or exploring. Who knows... maybe she needed some time away from us!"

Tiffany laughed. "We *are* a handful."

Tracy smiled weakly. "Yeah," she sighed, trying to relax her tense shoulders. "You are probably right. I am blowing this out of proportion."

Holly reached down to squeeze her hand. "You know what helps me when I am feeling off? Chores! Do you gals want to help me with some tasks around here? Maybe it will get your mind off of your worries for a while."

Tracy saw Isabella was about to decline, so she quickly spoke up. "Sure. What can we do for you?"

Holly grinned. "I am so happy to hear that. I was hoping you would say yes. I need some help gathering eggs from our chickens. I have some spare baskets in the closet. All you do is carefully reach in, grab the egg, and gently tuck it into the basket. Easy enough?"

"I can't wait," Tiffany beamed, her eyes sparkling with excitement. "I've always wanted to collect eggs. This will be fun."

Isabella yawned. "I think I am going to head back to the guest house," she announced to the group. "I'm exhausted, and I think I could use a nap. It's been a long weekend."

Holly, Tiffany, and Tracy exchanged looks as Isabella turned and left the house. "She's a bit of a princess," Tracy apologized to Holly. "But we are happy to help!"

Holly led them outside and over to the chicken coop, a large open air shack with dozens of chickens milling about. It reeked of animal feces, but the smells of hay and gasoline also crept into Tracy's nostrils.

"The nests are inside," she explained as she opened the door. They had to duck to fit inside. Tracy wondered how the Walker men ever managed to fit into the chicken house.

Inside, shelves containing nests of straw and hay lined the walls. Several chickens were on the floor, and a few climbed out of their homes when the women walked in.

Holly handed Tiffany a basket. "You first."

Tiffany gingerly reached into an empty nest and found a large brown egg. It was nearly as large as her palm, and it had four light blue speckles on the top.

"Perfect," Holly praised her. "And that is a beautiful egg. That will make for one tasty omelet. Now you, Tracy. Go on! It'll be fun, I promise."

Tracy held her breath as she plucked two medium eggs from the shelf below. They were not as pretty as Tiffany's eggs, but she liked how the texture of the shells felt in her hands. "What do you think?"

Holly took one of the eggs and examined it. "This will do," she decided as she gently set the egg in Tracy's basket. "You girls are naturals at this. Let's get the rest!"

As they hunted for eggs, Holly checked in regarding their stay. She asked how they had been enjoying the property and the town, and as Tiffany babbled on about how much she liked the country, Tracy thought about their unpredictable last few days.

"Tracy? How has your stay been? What do you think of our little haven?"

She saw Holly was watching her, and she forced herself to smile.

"It's so beautiful here," she complimented.

Holly's phone began to ring. "Sorry, let me silence the call," she apologized as she read the screen and then began to blush.

"It's okay," Tiffany told her. "Who is it?"

Holly shrugged. "No one," she smiled, though her pink cheeks betrayed her. "It's no one."

Tracy blinked at her. "Wait a minute. You are blushing, Holly."

"I see it, too!" Tiffany chimed in.

"Who was on the phone? Someone *special?*"

Holly's face was now a deep shade of red. She bit her lip. "I don't know what you're talking about," she replied nonchalantly.

"Yes, you do," Tiffany argued playfully. "Was that your boyfriend?"

The color drained from Holly's face. "You can't tell anyone, okay?"

Tracy pursed her lips. "What? Are you keeping him a secret or something?"

Holly put a hand on her heart. "I just don't want anyone to know. We've only been seeing each other a few months, and it's still very private."

Tracy watched as Holly tried to collect herself. "Does your family know you have a boyfriend?" she wondered aloud. "Do your brothers like him?"

Holly's lips flattened into a thin line. "They don't know about him," she revealed, looking down at her boots. "Look, Charles was an older brother to me, but also like a father. He was really strict, too. He never liked any of my boyfriends. He didn't even approve of my fiance. After years of him chasing away any guys who were interested, I learned that it was best to conduct my personal life in *private*."

"You were engaged?" Tiffany shrieked. "What happened? When was this?"

Holly sighed. "It was a long time ago, and it still hurts to think about," she began. "I was briefly engaged to my high school boyfriend, Tommy. He was sweet and funny, but Charles didn't think he was good enough for me. Tommy and I wanted to get married as soon as we graduated, but Charles refused to give us his blessing. I realized if I married

Tommy, I would lose my family. It was the hardest thing I ever did, but a month before the wedding, I called it all off. Tommy's heart was broken. He moved away and never looked back. I still think about him sometimes and wonder what happened to him."

Tracy shook her head. "I am so sorry," she said softly. "That must have been such a hard decision."

Holly's eyes filled with tears. "When my parents died, my siblings were all I had," she shared. "How could I have let Charles down and lose my family by getting married?"

"So now, you date in secret?" Tiffany asked. "Now that Charles is gone, will you ever tell your brothers and Molly about your boyfriend?"

Holly wiped her nose on her sleeve. "I don't know," she exhaled. "I've kept secrets from them for so long. I don't know if I even *could* tell them. What would they think?"

"That you are a normal woman in search of love, just like everyone else," Tracy told her. "You have every right to be happy and have a partner. Molly is married, and so is Derrick, so hopefully, they would understand."

Holly brushed a tear from her cheek. "You're right," she decided. "You're right, Tracy. I should just be honest with them. It's time to stop hiding my relationship. Hey, do you want to be the first people to see him? Wanna see a photo?"

Tiffany nodded excitedly. "YES!"

Holly scrolled through her phone and found a picture showing a tall blonde man kissing her cheek. "That's him."

"You are so cute together," Tracy complimented. "You look really happy."

"He makes me really happy." Holly gave a soft smile. "I like having you girls around," she divulged as she pulled Tracy and Tiffany in for a hug. "With Molly living so far away, I don't get enough girl time in my life. Your visit has been such a breath of fresh air for me."

"We'll have to keep in touch when we go home," Tiffany suggested. "You should come visit us."

Holly grinned. "I would love that," she agreed. "I would just *die* to get out of this town for a girls weekend of my own!"

19

After Tracy and Tiffany assisted Holly with the chores, the search for Aunt Rose resumed. Tracy felt calmer after Holly's reassurances, but she was still ready to know where her aunt had wandered off to. She led Tiffany outside to make a plan.

"I think we should split up," Tracy decided. "How about you walk into town, and I will do some searching around the property?"

"Deal," Tiffany agreed. "Call me if you find her."

"Right back atcha," Tracy told her.

She watched as Tiffany started walking down the gravel driveway, waiting until she disappeared from view to begin her own investigation. She wasn't sure where to begin, but something Holly said gave her an idea.

Tracy set off in search of the river. Her aunt loved being by water, and Tracy wondered if she had stumbled upon the river during a walk.

It took nearly a twenty-minute walk through the fields and into a thick forest to find the river. The sound of roaring water filled her ears as she approached, and Tracy admitted to herself that the incredible beauty of the dark blue water tearing over the boulders was worth the journey.

To her right, she spotted a deer and two babies carefully drinking from the river. Tracy was concerned for them; the currents looked strong, and the baby deer had such frail little legs. If they fell into the water, she wasn't sure they could make it out.

She peered over to her right, trying to see if her aunt could be spotted. She did not see her, and she decided to venture upstream.

Tracy navigated the tall grass and large rocks as she crept along the edge of the water. As she rounded a bend, she noticed the water was calmer, and the current appeared to weaken.

She nearly jumped out of her skin upon hearing a familiar sound. It was Aunt Rose's voice! Her aunt was singing an old hymn Tracy remembered from childhood. She followed the sound and was relieved when she saw her aunt sitting on a rock across the water.

"Aunt Rose!" she waved her arms. "What are you doing out here?"

Rose's eyes twinkled with delight. "I am enjoying the beautiful day!" she told her niece. "Come over here! There is someone I want you to meet."

Tracy rushed to a narrow spot in the river where she could easily jump from one bank to the other. She landed with a thud, falling on her knees, but she dusted herself off and raced toward her aunt.

She found Rose sitting with a middle-aged woman. The stranger had straight gray hair falling messily across her shoulders. She was dressed in a pair of khaki outdoor pants and an orange short sleeve button-up shirt, and a pair of brown work boots sat beside her.

"I am so happy I found you," Tracy told her aunt as she bent down to hug her. "We were all worried about you."

Rose lifted a brow. "Why the fuss? I told Isabella I was going for a walk," she said. "She was busy on her cell phone when I said it… I *knew* she wasn't really listening to me."

Tracy furrowed her brow. Of *course,* Isabella had not been helpful in this situation.

Rose gestured at the woman, who was staring at Tracy with curiosity. "Tracy, this is my new friend," her aunt introduced as the woman waved at her. "This is Mina Walker."

Tracy blinked several times. "Mina *Walker?*"

"That's me." The woman gave a half smile. "Charles' wife."

Tracy was shocked. Were the Walkers keeping *another* wife a secret? "Charles' *wife?*"

Mina shrugged. "Well, his widow, I guess."

Tracy looked over at her aunt. "How did you two meet?"

"Mina was out here fishing. I nearly scared her to death when I showed up here."

Mina glanced at Rose. "Not many people make it back here," she elaborated. "It was a surprise to find someone out by the river."

Tracy bit her lip. "I'm… sorry for your loss," she murmured, feeling uncomfortable.

Mina exhaled loudly. "Thanks. It's been a bit of a doozy."

"Mina thinks Charles died under suspicious circumstances," Rose informed her. "I was telling her all about your darling fiance, Warren, and the detective work he does. Mina wishes he could come out here and do some detective work for her."

"I don't think the police are taking this case seriously," Mina lamented, closing her eyes and leaning back to rest on her elbows. "Everyone in town knows Charles drank more than he should have, but something about it all just seems off to me…"

Tracy stared at her, thinking that *everything* about the mysterious Walker family seemed off to *her*.

"What makes you think the circumstances were suspicious?" she inquired, trying to sound casual.

Mina narrowed her eyes. "Charles was found with several bottles of booze nearby," she told them. "And as his wife, I know that *none* of the bottles found were anything he cared for. Charles was found with empty bottles of vodka and rum, but I *know* he was a whiskey man. He didn't like those other liquors. He wouldn't have drank himself to death with something he hated."

Tracy studied Mina's face. "Did you tell the police that?" she asked.

"They didn't listen to me," Mina complained. "Derrick and Abraham had already talked to the cops, and I think they fed the police a bunch of lies. By the time I went to the station to make a statement, the officer told me to just go home. He said I was hysterical."

Tracy looked at her aunt, and then back at Mina. "Who would kill your husband?" she asked, watching Mina's face crumble. "Why would anyone want Charles dead?"

Mina wrinkled her nose. "It was one of the siblings," she stated matter-of-factly. "I know it in my gut. Those greedy, good-for-nothing jerks wanted Charles dead so they could control the farm and the property."

Tracy cocked her head to the side. "Doesn't everyone own the property together?"

Mina sighed. "Yes, technically, but when their parents died, they made Charles the trustee of their estate. He made all final decisions about the farm, including every single financial detail. The others had no control, and those two brothers *hated* Charles for it."

Tracy could not believe what she was hearing. "You think it was Derrick or Abraham?"

"It could have been Molly or Holly too, I guess," Mina admitted. "But I don't think that it was. Molly lives her own life out East, and Holly and Charles were so close. Those boys, however, are trouble. And Derrick's wife, Monica, is a mess."

Rose patted Mina's arm. "You've been through so much…"

Mina went on. "A few years ago, there was a family meeting to discuss some financial trouble Charles had gotten us all into. He was a gambler, and he made a few mistakes, but Derrick and Abraham never got over it. Molly had to help for a few years, and finally, Derrick and Abraham demanded that Charles dissolve the trust and split the family fortune evenly."

"And he refused?"

Mina nodded. "You should have heard that nasty Monica screaming at us when Charles decided he was going to keep control of the trust. She called me names and swore that Charles would be sorry. I think she just wanted to take her share and leave Derrick. He runs around with other women, and Monica knows that."

Tracy struggled to process the new information. "So you think Monica, Derrick, and Abraham killed him?"

"Yes," Mina confirmed. "I think they staged it so it looked like an accident, and now, they are going to war with Molly over the trusteeship. She wants to be in charge, but the boys want to take their cuts."

Tracy heard the distress in Mina's voice. "Did you and Charles have a happy marriage?" she asked, wanting to learn more about the widow she didn't know existed until this point.

"We were so in love," Mina said, though her face betrayed her completely. Her jaw was tight, and Tracy saw her fists were clenched. "He was the love of my life."

Tracy wondered if the widow was hiding something and was throwing the Walker siblings under the bus to protect herself.

"I'm sorry you are going through this," Tracy finally said as she put her hands in her pockets. "Rose, I am going to head back to the house. Why don't you come with me?"

Her aunt refused. "I'm going to enjoy the fresh air for a while longer," she told her niece. "And I was enjoying getting to know Mina, too."

"Okay," Tracy agreed, though she wished her aunt would leave Mina and return with her. "Suit yourself. Be careful coming back."

Mina curled her fingers in a small wave. "Nice to meet you!"

"The pleasure was all mine," Tracy responded, turning to hurry away from the woods.

She thought about Mina's story as she walked through the woods. Was Mina telling the truth? Were the Walker siblings ruthless murderers who only cared about money? Why had no one in the family mentioned Mina *or* Monica to them? What other secrets were the Walkers keeping?

As Tracy turned a corner and emerged into the rolling fields, she saw two familiar figures in the distance. She squinted her eyes as she spotted Derrick and Abraham talking with a group of three men.

Tracy wanted to run away, but there was no good way to avoid them without bringing attention to herself. She held her head high and walked toward them, hoping to keep the interaction brief.

"Hey," Abraham greeted her as she approached the group. "Guys, this is one of our guests from out of town."

The three men were dressed in jeans, boots, and button up shirts. They nodded politely at her.

"How are you liking the area?" the shortest man asked.

She forced herself to smile. "It's… unforgettable," she claimed. "The town and the area are so pretty, and our hosts have been so kind, too."

Derrick winked at her before turning back to the men. "See? We Walker boys know how to impress," he joked as the group laughed. "I didn't pay her to say that, either."

The tallest stranger tipped his hat. "That's good to hear," he smiled at Tracy. He turned back to the Walkers. "Well, gentlemen, we'll be reaching out in the next week."

"Thank you for coming out," Abraham told him. "We appreciate your time."

They all shook hands, and soon, the men were walking back toward the main house.

"Who were those guys? Friends of yours?" she asked the Walker brothers.

They exchanged glances. "Not quite," Derrick admitted.

"Oh?"

Abraham sighed. "They are part of an investment group," he revealed. "They want to buy the property and develop it."

"They are looking to build a golf course and a high end neighborhood here," Derrick added. "The payout will be unreal."

She stared at them. "What do Holly and Molly think? I thought Holly wanted to keep running the guesthouse?"

Derrick closed his eyes. "Besides your group, no one has stayed here," he shared. "Holly's little hobby is a cute dream, but it just isn't working here."

"Neither is running a farm," Abraham chimed in. "This business isn't lucrative anymore and selling now will be the best option for us."

Derrick nodded. "Charles hated the idea of selling the land, but now that he's gone, we can make choices that are best for *everyone*. We just want our family to be secure and taken care of, and it seems like we can finally make that happen!"

She heard the excitement in his voice. "That's quite a plan," she said.

Tracy's thoughts began racing through her mind. Had the Walker brothers *murdered* their own brother to get him out of the way so they could take over the farm?

Abraham looked directly at her. "Please don't say anything to the girls," he requested. "Nothing is set in stone yet, and everyone is still upset about Charles."

"It just isn't a good time to bring all of this up," Derrick jumped in. "We're going to talk with the girls soon, but we need to get through the funeral, first."

Abraham's eyes were piercing, and she looked away.

"Okay," she promised. "I won't say a word."

The brothers high fived each other before glancing at Tracy. "It's gonna be great for all of us," Abraham told her. "Trust us."

"Of course," she lied. "I trust you."

20

"I'm so sorry, Tracy!" Tiffany exclaimed as Tracy walked into the guesthouse. "I looked all over town for Rose, but I didn't find her anywhere."

Tracy looked over at Isabella, who was sitting on the couch filing her nails.

"I *found* her, in case you cared," she said to Isabella.

Tiffany clapped her hands. "Where was she?"

"At the river," Tracy answered her, still staring at Isabella. "She said she told *you* she was going there, but you didn't listen."

Isabella placed the nail file on the end table beside her. "I didn't hear her say that," she defended herself.

Tiffany hugged Tracy. "I bet you are so relieved."

The chorus of a pop song began to play, and Isabella reached over to the end table and grabbed her phone. She giggled as she read the screen and then slipped the device into her pocket.

"Who was that?" Tracy asked her as she pulled away from Tiffany's embrace. "Who were you texting?"

Isabella frowned. "No one," she answered, crossing her arms over her chest. "I don't think that's your business."

The pop song played again, and Isabella grabbed her phone once more. Tracy noticed she was blushing.

"Who is it?" she repeated. "Who are you messaging?"

Isabella huffed. "The cute guy from the fishing place," she admitted. "Is that a problem?"

Tiffany glared at her. "This is a girls' trip," she declared. "You shouldn't be worried about guys when we are supposed to be focused on Tracy."

Isabella gave a sarcastic laugh. "Oh yeah? You weren't exactly focusing on Tracy when you were flirting with the Walker brothers at the bar."

"You were doing the same thing!"

They began to argue. Tracy did not want to listen to them, so she stepped outside and sat down on the porch swing.

She felt her phone vibrate and grinned when she realized Warren was calling her.

"Babe?" she answered. "Warren?"

"Are you okay?" he demanded to know. "Tracy, is everything okay?"

She paused for a moment as she registered the fear in his voice.

"Yes? I'm okay," she told him. "What's the matter? I've been missing you, babe. You have barely contacted me this weekend."

"We can talk about that later," he declared. "Tracy, I just saw on the news that someone *died* in the town where you are staying. Are you okay? Are the girls alright?"

Tracy heard the sound of girls giggling in the background. "Where are you?"

"We're at a pool party at Tao Beach Club," he shouted into the phone. "Sorry if you can't hear me. It's so loud here."

Tracy imagined her fiance at the pool sipping drinks and surrounded by bathing suit clad women. She gritted her teeth, determined to make *him* a bit jealous.

Tiffany walked outside and looked at her.

"It's Warren," she whispered before speaking into the phone again.

"We're fine," Tracy assured him, though she was not sure she herself believed it. "I'm having the best time. We've met some great people and gone out a lot. We've been at bars and danced and dressed up."

"That sounds…. nice," he commented. "Are you having fun?"

"Oh, so much fun," she fibbed. "Hey, we're about to get dressed up to go have drinks at a rooftop bar. After that, we are going to a club and then out dancing. I have to go. Talk to you soon. Love you."

"Tracy?" Warren called, but she hung up the phone.

Tiffany stared at her. "A rooftop bar? Clubbing? Why did you lie to him, Tracy?"

Tracy sighed. "He's barely called or texted this week, and I'm getting irritated. I wanted to make him a little jealous. I know that is immature, but I couldn't help myself."

Tiffany chuckled. "He loves you, Tracy," she reminded her. "He's busy with the guys. I wouldn't take it personally."

Tracy's shoulder slumped. "You're probably right," she acknowledged. "I should call him back and tell him the truth."

Before she could reach for her cell phone, Tiffany pointed at a woman walking over to the guest house. "Who is that?"

Tracy saw the long, straight hair and tall figure drawing closer. "Monica," she muttered.

"Who is Monica?" Tiffany asked.

"Long story," she replied as she stood up. "I'll be right back."

She strode over to meet Monica, who was waving at her.

"Hey," Monica smiled. She was holding a plate covered in tinfoil. "I made these for you and the girls."

She handed the plate to Tracy. "I hope you can have nuts. I made my famous cashew cookies."

Tracy looked down at the plate in her hands and then back at Monica. "That was so thoughtful. Thank you, Monica."

The woman nodded. "Of course. Everyone loves my cookies, so I thought you and your friends should enjoy them, too."

Before Tracy could reply, a truck drove into the driveway. Derrick Walker emerged with a worried look on his face.

"Honey," he greeted his wife as he walked over to them. "Have you met Tracy, our guest?"

Monica bobbed her head up and down. "Of course," she told him. "We met in town."

Derrick looked over at Tracy. "You've met my wife?" he asked weakly.

She raised an eyebrow. "Yep."

Monica peered at her husband. "What are *you* doing out here, honey?"

Derrick stuck his hands in his pockets. "I wanted to… check on the guesthouse. Holly had cleaners come after the fire and I wanted to make sure they did a good job."

Monica pursed her lips as she turned to look at Tracy. "The fire must have been so scary," she commented. "Thank goodness none of you were inside. I was sound asleep when everything happened, and I didn't even hear the sirens. Derrick told me what happened when he came in later. He stumbled in from the sports bar really, really late and filled me in."

Tracy looked at Derrick. "I thought you told me you went home right after we saw you at the country bar?"

Monica's eyes widened as she turned to her husband. "The *country* bar? You didn't mention running into the girls at the *country* bar."

"I didn't," he said. "I mean, I…"

Monica put her hands on her hips. "Did you lie to me?" she demanded to know. She drew herself up to her full height. "Derrick Walker, you had better have a good explanation. I thought we told each other everything!"

"We did," he sputtered, his face turning red. "We do."

Monica turned her attention to Tracy. "So you're saying you and your friends saw my husband out at the bar? The sports bar?"

"No," Tracy shook her head. "The country bar."

Monica's eyes turned into thin slits as the anger consumed her. "You told me you would never set foot in there again, you two-faced liar! I am going to *kill* you."

Derrick's wife balled her hands into fists, and with a growl, she lunged toward her husband.

21

Derrick sprang into action. He pulled his wife into his arms and held her tightly, preventing her from hitting him.

"Baby, it's a misunderstanding," he promised as she tried to wriggle out of his grasp. "I behaved! I didn't even talk to Gabby."

"Who is Gabby?" Tracy asked, confused by what was happening.

"The waitress he kissed when he was drunk last New Year's Eve," Monica spat as she pulled away from her husband.

"It was one time," he pleaded with her. "It was one kiss. It didn't mean anything."

Monica's face turned red. "You promised you would never go there again. What else are you lying about? What other promises are you breaking?"

Derrick's eyes widened. "Baby, I have a good explanation," he insisted as Monica's lip quivered.

"You're cheating," she accused him as Tracy watched in horror. "Tell me the truth."

Derrick's hands were shaking as he tried to reach for his wife. "Baby, the truth is that I… I was at the country bar to buy our anniversary present."

Monica scoffed. "Oh? You wanted to buy me a present from a *bar?*"

He shook his head. Tracy wondered what he was going to say.

"I bought you *tickets*, babe," he told her as a second truck pulled up and the other Walker brother popped out. "Look, Abe is here. Ask Abraham. He'll tell you the truth."

Monica turned to her brother-in-law and stared at him. "Tell me the truth," she ordered as Abraham looked at his brother. "What is going on?"

Derrick pasted a smile on his lips. "Bro, I was just telling Monica what we were up to at the country bar… how I was only there to buy her tickets for the Gladys Miller concert."

"Right!" Abraham chimed in, though Tracy could tell he was lying. "Derrick tried to get the tickets online, but they were sold out. He saw that they were selling them at the bar, so he begged me to come with him to get them for you."

Monica studied their faces. "Is this true?"

Abraham grinned. "He's a romantic," he laughed as he reached over and gave his brother a playful swat on the shoulder. "He wanted to surprise you with the tickets."

Derrick nodded earnestly, and Monica's face broke. She smiled at her husband. "That was so thoughtful of you."

Derrick grabbed her and kissed her on the lips. "Anything for my baby," he promised as their lips broke apart.

Monica nodded at her brother-in-law. "Thanks for helping him out," she told Abraham.

Derrick took her hand. "We should get going," he urged his wife. "See you two later."

"Enjoy the cookies!" Monica called out as she followed her husband to his truck.

Tracy watched them, and as Monica climbed into the vehicle, Derrick shot Tracy a nasty look.

They drove away, and she looked at Abraham. "Why is he lying to his wife?" she asked. "And why did you back him up?"

Abraham stared at her. "Do you have any siblings?" he asked.

"No."

"Then you won't get it," he shrugged. "We're all each other has. Besides, Derrick is a good guy. He's made some mistakes in his marriage, but one night out at a bar isn't worth Monica going crazy over."

Tracy bit her lip. "Derrick lied to her without hesitation," she said slowly. "Does he lie a lot?"

"No," Abraham snapped at her. "What are you trying to say about my brother?"

"Did Derrick lie to Charles, too? Or Holly?"

Abraham got closer to her, leaning down and getting in her face. "What are you trying to say about my brother?" he repeated.

Tracy did not flinch. "Maybe your brother was in more trouble than he let on," she suggested as he glowered at her. "Maybe your brother isn't just lying about his marriage…"

Abraham's nose was only inches from hers. She could smell his breath, and her stomach curled as he moved even closer.

"That's enough," he warned her. "That's enough from you. You stay out of our business, and the second your stay is over, get off our property. I don't want to see any of you people again, and that's a *warning*."

22

As Abraham walked away, Tracy began shaking. Both Walker brothers seemed unhinged. She was rattled by the threatening interaction, and she could not believe they had blatantly lied to Monica.

She started thinking about Charles Walker. Charles had his demons, but from what Holly had said, it sounded like Charles wanted to peacefully run the farm and keep things the way they had been for hundreds of years. Tracy wondered about Mina Walker, too. She had spoken poorly of her brothers-in-law, but was she lying, too? Could Mina Walker be in cahoots with Derrick and Abraham?

Tracy wandered over to the massive barn where Charles had died. She glanced around, making sure no one was around to see her before she stepped inside.

The barn was huge. With dark wood finishings, stalls filled with healthy young horses, and the smell of hay permeating the air, it felt like Tracy had been transported back to the

19th century when the original Walkers had arrived on the land.

She peeked over at the spot where Charles had been found. A few pieces of yellow caution tape were wrapped around the corner, but nothing else was preventing anyone from interfering with the scene.

"Excuse me?"

She jumped as a man's voice interrupted her thoughts. She spun around to find an older man in a pair of overalls smiling at her.

"Can I help you?"

"I hope so," he told her. "I was scheduled to come out to take a look at the sliding door, but I got a call on my way out here and was told the job was done. I took a peek at the door, and it still needs to be repaired. Is the owner around? I'd like to talk to them about it."

Tracy nodded, but before she could speak, Holly's voice rang through the barn.

"Tracy? What are you doing here?"

Tracy smiled. "Just looking around," she shared. "This gentleman was looking for you, though. He's here to fix the door."

Holly shook her head. "I'm sorry, but I called and canceled the appointment," she told him. "We have some family things going on, and now isn't a good time."

He furrowed his brow. "Are you sure? I can have it done in a few minutes. I won't be a bother."

"No," Holly refused. "Please go. I will call back another time."

He wrinkled his nose. "Suit yourself."

The women watched as the repairman saw himself out.

"What was that all about?" Tracy inquired as he slammed the door shut.

Holly closed her eyes. "It's my fault," she groaned. "The door needs to be fixed, and I off-handedly mentioned it to Abraham. He scheduled the repairman to come out, but when I found out, I canceled the appointment."

"Why?"

"That man has done work here before, and he's done a terrible job," Holly explained. "He's a buddy of my brother's, and Abraham keeps giving him jobs to do. Charles would be furious. The last time that guy came out, he broke our stained glass window in the bathroom and didn't bother putting it back together."

"I'm sorry that happened," Tracy told her. "It must be hard to manage so many different opinions and ideas around here."

"You have no idea," Holly frowned. "And with Molly in town, it only intensifies everything. I love my sister, but she always shows up here and expects to be in charge."

Tracy blinked. "It must be so stressful to have all of this going on while planning a funeral."

"I just wish they would find the killer," Holly fretted. "The word around town is that Charles was murdered, and I don't think things will get back to normal until the killer is caught."

Tracy took a deep breath. "Do you have any guesses?" she asked directly. "Or any hunches about a motive?"

Holly stared at her. "Why? Why are you asking?"

"I… just wanted to offer support," Tracy replied with a hint of defensiveness in her voice. "I feel so bad that you are going through what you are going through, and I wish I could do more. My fiance, Warren, is a detective, and I wish I could just snap my fingers and get him here to help you solve this case."

Holly perked up. "He's a detective?"

"The best of the best," Tracy boasted. "He solved several cold cases last year, and one even led to a kidnapped little boy being returned home to his family."

"He sounds amazing," Holly told her. "You are so lucky to have a detective in the family."

Tracy watched the sadness creep into Holly's eyes. "Do you want me to call him?" she offered. "I could give him a call and see if he has any tips."

Holly smiled earnestly. "That would be incredible," she decided. "Let's give him a call right now!"

23

Tracy pulled out her cell phone, but before she could dial the number, Holly snatched the device.

"Is this him?" she asked, pointing at the screen's background photo of Warren and Tracy holding hands in front of the gazebo where they had gotten engaged.

"Yep. That's Warren."

Holly giggled. "He is so handsome! You make such a lovely couple."

Suddenly, she stumbled, and the phone flew out of her hands. Tracy tried to catch it, but her cell phone shattered at it hit the concrete floor.

Holly gasped. "I am so sorry," she apologized as she and Tracy bent down to collect the pieces of the broken screen. "Be careful. I don't want you to get hurt."

Tracy groaned as she tried to turn on her broken phone. It lit up, but it was impossible to see anything on the screen.

"I'll send you money to replace it," Holly sighed. "I am so sorry. I am such a clutz."

Just then, the barn door opened and Molly Walker strutted in. She was wearing a pair of tight white capri pants, a blue and white floral top, and a pair of embellished sandals. She looked wildly out of place amidst the barn's rustic interior, and she frowned as she saw the shards of glass on the floor.

"What happened?"

Holly and Tracy stood up. "I dropped her phone," Holly revealed.

"Hi, Tracy," Molly greeted her before turning back to her sister. "Speaking of the phone, there is a call for you at the house. Can you come take it?"

"Who is it?"

Molly blinked. "I don't know, but they said it is urgent."

Holly glanced over at Tracy. "I'm sorry," she apologized again. "I will make it up to you."

She then turned and bounded out of the barn. Molly shook her head. "That girl has always been so clumsy," she commented. "Sorry about your phone."

"It's just another casualty of this weekend," Tracy joked before seeing Molly's eyes narrow. "Oh, my gosh. I am so sorry. That was so inappropriate to say."

Molly brushed her off. "It's fine, it's fine."

A small twinkle of light hit Tracy's face, and she realized it was from Molly's wedding ring.

"Will your husband be joining you for the funeral?" she asked Molly. "I assume he's back in New York?"

Molly nodded. "He has a really busy schedule, so he likely won't come out for another few days," she noted.

"How long have you two been married?"

"Oh, years," Molly laughed. "We're just a pair of old married people, now. He's still got it, though; he's very handsome and works out almost daily. It's really attractive."

"Can I see a photo?" Tracy asked, hoping to stay on Molly's good side.

"Sure."

Molly pulled out her phone. "Here we are on our wedding day," she narrated as she handed the phone to Tracy.

Tracy felt sick. In her slinky white satin dress, Molly was a stunning bride. The groom, however, was a familiar face; Tracy recognized the tall blonde man as the guy from the photo Holly had shown her.

"This is your husband?"

"Of fifteen years," Molly gushed. "Isn't he a doll?"

Tracy's heart pounded as she nodded weakly. "So handsome."

The barn door opened and Holly returned.

"Who called?" Molly asked. "They sounded serious."

Holly rolled her eyes. "It was the town librarian," she replied, her voice oozing with annoyance. "She has been bugging me about making a donation in Charles' name. I've avoided her calls for days."

Molly's eyes widened. "That is so rude. We haven't even had the funeral yet. Why is she harassing you? Do you want me to go down there and give her a piece of my mind? You know I will."

Holly shrugged. "You don't have to…"

Molly nodded. "I will. I can tell it upset you. I will go over to the library and make sure she knows her manners the next time she talks to you."

Molly dramatically threw open the barn door and left. Holly chuckled. "She's a spitfire," she observed as Holly stared at her. "What's wrong? You look like you've seen a ghost."

Before she could stop herself, Tracy shared what she had seen on Molly's phone. "Are you having an affair with your sister's husband?" she asked gently. "Holly, how long has it been going on?"

Holly's nostrils flared. "Don't tell anyone," she demanded as Tracy took a step back. "Please, you don't understand. Ugh. I wish you had just minded your own business, Tracy."

Tracy gave her a soft smile. "Help me understand?"

Holly shook her head. "It's love, Tracy," she began. "We didn't mean for it to happen, but it did."

The barn door opened and two farm hands walked in, laughing and joking as they went over to the first horse stall and began to clean it.

"Come with me," Holly said quietly. "Let's go somewhere quiet, where we can have some privacy. I'll tell you everything."

Holly led Tracy to a remote corner of the farm. They went through the woods, over the river, and across the fields to a derelict structure overlooking a lush valley.

"This was one of the barns our great-grandparents built," Holly told her as they walked inside.

The roof was caving in, and the windows did not have any glass in them. Bugs crawled across the walls, and the smell of animal feces made Tracy cringe.

"I come here to think sometimes," Holly explained. "I imagine what life was like when my ancestors moved here. No one comes out here anymore, and this is a place where I can get away from all the trouble."

She sat down on the ledge of an old stall and beckoned Tracy to join her. "So… what do you want to know?"

Tracy took a deep breath. "Why are you seeing Molly's husband? Does she know?"

"Of course, she doesn't know." Holly hung her head. "I don't want to hurt her. It just… happened. He loves me, though, Tracy. He comes out here every month to see me. It's real for us. He was going to tell Molly, and we were going to run away together, but…"

Tracy studied her face. "But what?"

Her eyes flashed with rage. "Charles found out."

Tracy's jaw dropped. "Oh, my goodness. How?"

"He walked in on us at the guesthouse," Holly admitted, moving her fingers to nervously tug on her hair. "There was no mistaking what we had been up to. He knew what had been going on, and he demanded that I end it."

Holly reached into her backpack and pulled out a water bottle. "Thirsty?" she offered Tracy. "It gets stuffy out here."

Tracy nodded gratefully and took a swig. She nearly choked as the bitter liquid hit her throat, and she spat out most of the drink on the ground.

"What's wrong?" Holly asked innocently.

"That was awful," Tracy moaned. "What was in that drink?"

Holly's lips curled upward into a smile. "It's an old family recipe," she informed Tracy.

"Ugh," Tracy gagged.

Holly rose from her seat and stared at Tracy. "You've asked a lot of questions," she observed as Tracy tried to clear her throat. "You seem to have taken a real interest in my family."

Tracy shrugged. "I've always been a curious person."

"Maybe a little too curious," Holly said darkly. "We both know why we're here, Tracy. Honestly, I'm shocked that you followed me back here. I thought you were a little wiser than that."

Tracy was confused. "What are you talking about?" she asked as Holly reached into her pocket.

"Oh, don't play the fool right now," Holly laughed. "We both know what happened, don't we? But after this, only one of us will go back to the farm."

Holly pulled a shiny revolver out of her pocket and pointed it at Tracy.

"What? Holly?! What are you doing?"

Holly drew closer to her. Tracy could hear her own heart beating as Holly leveled the gun to be right in front of Tracy's nose.

"I can't have you giving away my secret," Holly sighed. "You know too much."

"About your boyfriend? Holly, I don't care. Molly isn't my sister. I won't tell. It doesn't matter to me."

Holly looked shocked. "What?"

"Your boyfriend? Isn't that why you are upset? Holly, I would never judge you. I don't know Molly, and I don't know how it was to grow up in this family, but I promise that I don't care what you do in your personal life."

Holly was clearly taken aback. "Tracy, you are a good actress," she finally said. "You really missed your calling in the theater."

"What?" Tracy stuttered. "What?"

Holly released her arm and held the gun by her side. "Don't play dumb," she warned Tracy. "I know you know about what really happened to Charles. You've been sniffing around in our business all weekend, and I know you've figured it out."

Tracy clenched her hands in frustration. "Figured WHAT out?" she shouted, fearing Holly had lost her mind.

"That I killed my brother," Holly confessed in an even voice. "That I killed Charles and am not the least bit sorry about it."

Tracy was stunned. "You killed Charles?" she whispered as Holly nodded. "Because he found out about you and Molly's husband?"

Holly shook her head. "That was the final straw," she revealed, crossing her arms and starting to pace around the wooden floor. "When our parents died, Charles ruled this farm with an iron fist. He had his own issues, but for the most part, we got along."

"So why did you kill him?"

Holly whipped her head around to stare at her. "Because he stole my first chance at love," she told her. "I ended my engagement because of him. I lost the love of my life. When I fell for my boyfriend, I decided I was done letting my brother and my family rule my life."

"Why did you have to kill him?" Tracy wondered as Holly's lip began to quiver. "Couldn't you two have just run away together? You could have left the farm and started over somewhere else."

"This farm is my birthright," Holly declared as she held her head high. "It belongs to *all* of us, but Charles was the trustee. He had control over the finances and the property, and if I had left, I would have been penniless. How could I start a new life with my boyfriend if I had nothing? His money is locked up in a prenup with his wife, so we would have both had nothing to our names."

"So you killed your oldest brother?"

Holly narrowed her eyes. "Think about how you feel about your fiance," she offered. "Do you love him?"

"Of course."

"Do you love him so much that you would kill to be with him?"

Tracy exhaled. "I don't know if I can answer that."

Holly glowered at her. "I can. I love my man so much that I risked it all to be with him, and now we are so close to our dreams coming true. I will not let a nosy out of towner ruin it all for me."

Holly raised the gun and pointed it at Tracy. "Here's how it's gonna go," she revealed as Tracy's body shook with fear. "The drink you just swallowed? It's a poisonous little concoction that will knock you out in the next few minutes. You spat out so much, though, and I think I am going to have to finish the job myself."

Tracy held up her hands in defeat. "Please," she begged Holly. "Please don't do this. I can keep my mouth shut. I won't tell anyone. I can get the girls out of here and we can leave tonight. Please, Holly. Please."

Holly scoffed. "How can I trust you? It's all over town that you've been poking your nose around our business."

"I didn't tell on Derrick," Tracy countered. "When his *wife* was asking questions about his whereabouts."

Holly cackled. "I don't think keeping Derrick's indiscretions a secret and hiding a murder are exactly comparable…."

She pointed the gun at Tracy and fingered the trigger. "It'll be quick," she promised. "I've killed hundreds of farm animals and hunted for years. You won't feel a thing."

Tracy held up her hands in a feeble attempt to shield herself. "Please," she begged as she fell to her knees. "Please don't do this. There has to be another way."

Holly took a step forward, but the heel of her boot caught the end of the stall and sent her plunging forward toward Tracy. Seizing her moment, Tracy reached for the gun and tucked it into her belt. She rose from her feet and turned to run from the barn, but Holly was right behind her.

"Stop!" Holly screamed as she grabbed Tracy's hair. "Give that back to me."

The gun fell out of Tracy's belt and clattered onto the floor. Both women dove for it, and Tracy used her fingernails to dig into Holly's face.

"OUCH!" she shrieked as drops of blood trickled down her cheeks. "You are gonna be sorry for that!"

Tracy elbowed Holly in the stomach, but Holly swiftly kicked her in the knees. She pinned Tracy to the ground and straddled her, squeezing her legs tightly around Tracy's torso. Tracy bucked and wriggled, but she could not escape Holly's grasp.

Holly quickly let go of Tracy's right wrist and snatched the gun from the floor. She held it over Tracy's throat, and Tracy could feel the cold barrel pressing against her skin.

"I didn't want to do this," Holly muttered. "But you've left me no choice."

Tracy watched as Holly's fingers stroked the trigger. She closed her eyes, imagining her family and friends and wishing she could transport herself back a few days in time before she had ever left on her stupid trip.

"Three... two..." Holly counted.

"ONE."

BOOM. A loud noise filled the room, and all Tracy saw was darkness.

25

All Tracy could see was a bright light. She felt warm and sleepy, and it was as if she was floating.

"Is this what it feels like to be dead?" she wondered as the light became even brighter. "Am I on the other side?"

The light flashed and overcame her, and Tracy shuddered. She blinked several times and realized she was in a hospital bed.

"You're awake!" a familiar voice cried out. Tracy saw Tiffany, Rose, and Isabella were seated next to her bed.

"I'm alive?" she asked. Her mouth was dry, and her head was aching.

Rose nodded and reached to take Tracy's hand. "You are," she confirmed. "The police showed up at the barn before that crazy woman hurt you."

Tracy felt her stomach churn. "She *did* hurt me," she corrected her aunt. "She poisoned me."

Tiffany gestured at an IV bag next to Tracy's bed. "The doctors are flushing it out of you," she informed her. "They found you right in the nick of time. They said if they hadn't started treating you when they did, you would have died within the hour."

Tracy groaned. Her entire body felt sore, and she wondered how long she had been sleeping.

"How did they find me at that nasty old barn?" she asked. "It's a miracle that *anyone* managed to get out there."

Rose nodded. "The other sister, Molly? She led the police out there."

"What? How did she know to do that?"

Isabella's face brightened. "The Walker family sure has a lot of drama," she shared in a gossipy tone. "After the police left, we heard her screaming about what happened. She overheard her sister telling you about the *affair* Holly was having with Molly's husband, and she had a gut feeling that Holly was up to something even worse."

"Oh my gosh," Tracy moaned. "Molly must be devastated."

"She's angrier than the devil," Rose mentioned. "She threw her wedding ring into the river and was shouting something about a prenup. It was ugly."

Tiffany held up her cell phone. "It's Warren," she shared. "Do you want to talk to him? Rose called and told him what happened, and he's been trying to get ahold of you."

"Holly broke my phone," Tracy muttered. "Can you put him on speakerphone?"

Tiffany pushed a button. "Yep! Warren? You're on speakerphone."

Warren's frantic voice filled the room. "Honey? Are you okay? Tracy? Tracy?"

"I'm here," she responded, her voice hoarse. "I love you."

"I love you, too."

She could tell he had been crying. "How is your party?"

Warren cleared his throat. "It doesn't matter. I'm flying out to be with you tonight."

"What?"

"My bachelor party doesn't matter," he assured her. "Your safety and health is the only thing that matters to me, babe. I'll be there by midnight."

She shook her head. "Don't come," she urged him. "I am going to be just fine, and I don't want to spoil your plans."

"Besides," Isabella jumped in. "Tracy has plans after this. Don't come, Warren."

Rose took the phone from Tiffany. "I'll speak with him," she advised. "Tracy, say goodbye."

"Bye, hon. Love you."

"I love you, too."

Rose disappeared into the hallway and came back a few minutes later with Marty, the police officer.

"How is the patient?" he asked cheerfully as Tracy gave a weak wave. "I told you to be careful around this town, Tracy."

"I guess I am just a magnet for trouble," she sighed. "Rose, is Warren okay?"

"He'll be just fine. I assured him you are in good hands." She turned to the officer. "It's nice of you to come check on my niece," Rose complimented him.

He pulled a notebook out of his vest. "I'm actually here on official duty," he explained. "Tracy, if you are up to it, I need to ask you a few questions about what happened with Holly."

"She is resting," Rose protested, but Tracy waved her hand to dismiss her.

"I can talk," she agreed, carefully sitting up. "What do you want to know?"

Marty asked about the old barn, Holly's confession, and the weapon. Though her mind was foggy and her body hurt, Tracy answered as best as she could.

"Officer," Rose interjected after thirty minutes of questioning. "I think that is enough. Tracy is exhausted and went through so much yesterday."

Tracy didn't realize she had been asleep for nearly twenty-hour hours. "I'm okay," she insisted. "Actually, officer, I have a question for *you.*"

"Let's have it," he nodded.

"Were the others involved?"

He stared at her. "The others?"

"The other Walker family members. Derrick, Mina, Abraham, Monica, and Molly. Did they play a part in the murder?"

He chuckled. "The Walkers are a troubled family," he began, leaning back in his chair. "Which I am sure you and your friends have realized. Between their greed, indiscretions, and selfishness, the Walker family could have their own soap opera."

Tiffany bit her lip. "But did they help Holly kill her brother?"

"While each Walker had every reason to want Charles dead, my team and I have every reason to believe that Holly Walker acted alone," he revealed to the group. "Derrick, Abraham, Molly, and their spouses detested Charles, but they all have solid alibis."

Isabella wrinkled her nose. "Then who tried to burn down the guest house?"

"Holly," Marty answered. "She stored her poison in the guesthouse and was desperate to cover her tracks."

"But she was with Rose that night," Tracy interjected.

"For a while… Rose, do you remember anything about when you had tea with Holly?"

Rose closed her eyes. "I dozed off for a few minutes when Holly slipped off to the powder room," she confessed. "But I thought I was just a little tired. She was only gone a few minutes."

"That's all it took," he explained. "Holly wanted to get rid of the evidence. She hurried down to the guesthouse and lit a match…"

Tracy was confused. "But why did she try to kill *me*?"

"She thought *you* had caught on to her," he told them. "Holly was convinced that you had put the pieces together. She knew you were inquisitive, and she believed you had figured her out."

"I really had no idea," Tracy giggled in spite of herself. "I thought Monica and Derrick did it. They seemed so impulsive and immature."

Marty chuckled. "I thought it was Mina and Abraham," he disclosed to them. "Rumor has it that those two dated for a while when they were in high school. I wondered if Mina just hated her husband and wanted to run off with Abraham. Little did I know I was tracking the wrong Walker."

Isabella let out a loud sigh. "It's official. This has been the worst bachelorette party imaginable. I totally failed you as a friend, Tracy."

Tiffany looked heartbroken. "This sure wasn't what we hoped for, Tracy."

Tracy blinked at her friends. "Wait a minute," she stopped them. "I'm alive. I made it! We might not be leaving with a lot of fun stories, but I am leaving here with my *life*."

"That's the spirit," Marty nodded at her as he stood up. "My team and I will be in touch about the investigation and potentially, a trial for Holly. Take good care and rest up, you hear?"

"You bet," Tracy agreed.

He said goodbye and left the four women to themselves. Rose smoothed Tracy's hair out of her face.

"I'll make this up to you, Tracy," Isabella declared as she pulled out her cell phone. "I will make sure you have the weekend of your dreams."

Tracy's eyes widened. "Really, I think we've all had enough," she murmured.

Isabella looked up at her. "Trust me, dear. I've made some plans for when you are released. You are going to get the weekend you *deserve* at last. I am *dying* to tell you all about it, but it's going to be a surprise."

Tracy glanced up at her aunt. "Should I be worried?"

Aunt Rose bent down and kissed her on the forehead. "This time, there is nothing to worry about," she promised. "I swear on my life that there is nothing to worry about."

26

"Would you like me to top off your drink, Miss?" asked a uniformed waiter holding a bottle of champagne.

Tracy nodded. "That would be lovely," she agreed, giggling as he filled her glass to the top.

She held it to her lips and took a long sip. "So good," she told him. "What is this? I've never had a mimosa like this before."

"It's our famous spicy peach mimosa," he informed her. "Enjoy."

Tracy took another long drink, enjoying the sensation of the bubbles against her lips. She yawned, stretching out across the chaise lounge where she had been resting for the past hour.

Tiffany reached over from her own chair and tapped Tracy on the shoulder. "Look, Isabella is on the prowl again," she rolled her eyes as they saw Isabella smiling and talking with a waiter.

They were mistaken though; Isabella was placing an order for lunch, and she returned moments later holding a tray of tacos, guacamole, and several bowls of rice.

"This is the life," Tracy remarked as the sun warmed her cheeks. "This is exactly what I hoped my special weekend would be like."

The day she had been released from the hospital, Isabella had driven them to the regional airport. They flew to San Diego, and from there, were met by a driver who whisked them away to a five-star resort in La Jolla, an upscale beach town just north of the city.

"It's too much," she had told Isabella, but Isabella stopped her.

"I had a million credit card points from my old job," she explained as they were shown to their ocean-view suite on the first floor. Rose and Tiffany were settling into the adjoining room.

"And it was the least I could do. I got us into that mess in Greenhithe Falls, and it was my job to give you the weekend of your dreams….so here we are."

Tracy threw her arms around her friend. "Thank you," she whispered.

"I'm sorry," Isabella stopped her, pulling away from Tracy's embrace. "I was spoiled and selfish all weekend. I am a little jealous of you, Tracy, and that ugly side of me spilled out."

Tracy was shocked. "You are jealous of *me*? You are so smart and well-traveled and you look like a movie star. How could you be jealous of me?"

"You have an aunt who loves you, good friends, and a loving fiance," Isabella sighed, looking down at her shoes with an embarrassed look on her face. "You are confident and fun, and you never let anything stop you from getting what you want."

Tracy felt a pang of sympathy for her friend. "You could have those things, too," she said gently. "Happiness is for *everyone*, Isabella. You just have to find it, or create it for yourself."

"Yeah," her friend shrugged, still not meeting her gaze. "You're right, I guess."

"Hey," Tracy murmured. "Look at me."

Isabella shyly looked into Tracy's eyes. "Yeah?"

"You are beautiful and fun and worthy of love," Tracy promised her. "I love you, and I know someday, we'll be celebrating your bachelorette weekend when *you* find the love of your life. It's only a matter of time…and who knows? Maybe the love of your life is here in La Jolla. He could be lounging by the pool right now!"

Isabella laughed. "You think so?"

"Let's get changed and go find out," Tracy winked.

The End

AFTERWORD

Thank you for reading Lavender and a Messy Blunder! I really hope you enjoyed reading it as much as I had writing it!

If you have a minute, please consider leaving a review on Amazon or the retailer where you got it.

Many thanks in advance for your support!

CARNATIONS AND DEADLY FIXATIONS

CHAPTER 1 SNEAK PEEK

ABOUT CARNATIONS AND DEADLY FIXATIONS

Released: August, 2019
Series: Book 1 – Fern Grove Cozy Mystery Series
Standalone: Yes
Cliff-hanger: No

Tracy Adams had three things going for her in her just-above-average boring life namely:

1. A good job

2. A good job… that she liked

3. A good job that she liked… and paid VERY well

When she lost her job and had to move back to the small town where she grew up, it seemed like her life had lost all purpose. Helping at her aunt's floundering floral shop seemed like the perfect distraction before she decided what to do next.

When her aunt's competition, a nasty and egotistical know-it-all is found dead, the rumor mill in Fern Grove goes into overdrive. With an important piece of evidence linking Tracy to the scene of the crime, she becomes a person of interest in the murder investigation. This leaves her feeling vulnerable and confused.

Moving back to Fern Grove was meant to be the start of a new life but this murder mystery is fast ending what has hardly begun. Will she keep her wits and piece the clues that will lead her to the killer?

CHAPTER 1 SNEAK PEEK

Tracy Adams popped her work apron over her head as she made her way out of the back of *In Season*, the small, but established flower shop her aunt, Rose Bishop had founded with her husband, Frank, many years ago. In the few moments of peace and quiet that she knew would be short-lived once her aunt arrived, Tracy sipped at her coffee and her mind wandered. Tracy would never have imagined that her life would have taken the sharp detour it had. At thirty-eight, and with the trajectory that her once burgeoning professional life had been on, helping run a somewhat floundering florist shop had sure not been on her menu. She had landed her dream job right out of The University of Portland, doing event planning for CMB Capital, an up and coming bank in Portland, Oregon. Her future looked as bright as could be imagined until some questionable speculations by the senior management team put the high flying financial newcomer in jeopardy.

Once decisions had been made, it was like this rolling tide that everyone could see coming, but were unable to stem.

She observed as colleagues and friends at CMB were told their positions had been deemed "redundant". Tracy despised all forms of euphemistic language, but this term especially raised her ire; like calling the blow that you were about to be laid off could be softened by this word. She held her breath and prayed she would survive the cutbacks, but in her heart, she knew her position as an event planner was most likely not an essential role for CMB's survival.

The days went by and Tracy actually began to believe she had somehow been spared. But then one morning her boss, William Atherton, the man who had recruited her out of her undergraduate program, came with the bad news she had been dreading. Though he promised she would be one of the last of the furloughed staff to be dismissed, due to her great work since coming onboard and her undying loyalty to CMB, it was just empty words. She was sure Atherton had been sincere in his pronouncement to her, as she could see on his face when her dismissal came down, that the decision had most likely come from above him.

So here she was, back in her small hometown of Fern Grove once more, looking out the window at *In Season*, the family business she had known as a child. After losing her job at CMB, it had been a struggle, for Tracy as well as a lot of others, to recover and acquire new professional positions. She was starting to get a little frantic as to what she would do and how she was going to pay her bills when her Aunt Rose inquired as to whether she would be interested in coming to the florist shop and helping her out. Rose had become like a mother figure to Tracy ever since her mother, Madeline, Rose's sister, had died suddenly in a traffic accident when Tracy was just fifteen. Rose and her husband had founded and grown *In Season* from scratch and it had, over time, become very popular in Fern Grove. Once a successful businesswoman in Fern Grove, the death of Frank was the catalyst that led to Rose neglecting the business. That, plus having her own kids move out of Fern Grove and then away from Oregon as well, had dampened her drive and though still respected in town, Rose was just feeling fatigued and mowed down by the circumstances in her life.

During a call with her aunt one day, Tracy had innocently inquired as to how things were going at *In Season*, as she knew Rose was struggling with all the downturns she had encountered as of late. She could hear the sadness in her voice and though she was concerned, she had never ever considered helping out until Rose just came out with it.

"I don't know, Tracy…" Rose said with a heavy sigh, "some days I just do not know…"

"Aunt Rose?" Tracy asked as her aunt's voice just trailed off without any seeming direction.

"It's just not the same without Frank anymore. Flowers are not moving the way they used to, and some days it just seems too overwhelming, you know?"

"Maybe time for some changes?"

"Maybe…maybe…you still looking for a job?"

"You know I am, Aunt Rose."

"You had a really high-flying position over at CMB before they nearly went under doing corporate events, seminars and job fairs…things like that, right?"

"Yes…"

"Maybe with that experience, you could join me and help me turn this place around."

Tracy paused as she had not been expecting this. However, there was a part of her that was excited at the prospect of remolding *In Season* back into what it had once been…maybe even better! She smiled over the phone, welcoming the challenge to bring some 'big business' concepts and strategies she had learned to a small business. Without any more hesitation, her brain was already bubbling with innovative strategies and modern plans for action. Her only real hurdle, she knew, was going to be her aunt.

She knew Rose was still stuck in the mindset she and Frank had instituted when they had begun when Tracy was just a little girl. Times were changing all around, even in Fern Grove, and the way people were looking at and purchasing flowers was evolving as well. But Rose seemed resistant to change with the times. Part of it was her age, Tracy knew, and she was sure Rose might be a bit intimidated by how technology was impinging on everything these days—something that was likely to be as foreign to her aunt as waking up one day and discovering she now had three heads. Tracy was sure she could overcome it, just as she had other similar instances in her life.

Having lost her husband and then having her kids move far away, Tracy knew, was part of her aunt's inertia as well. It had taken the fire out of her belly after she had been so successful. And all of this together was contributing to the downturn in revenue at *In Season*. The last time Tracy had been to the shop she was struck by just how frumpy and old-fashioned the interior appeared in relation to the new shops that had opened around town. Tracy readily agreed to help her out; somewhat out of an obligation to her aunt who had caught her when she was collapsing after her mother's demise, but also it was just her nature to want to help out when she was asked. However, the one stipulation was that

Rose allow Tracy to institute some serious changes to the shop—ones that would bring *In Season* into the 21st century. Rose reluctantly conceded, but in the tone of her voice, Tracy could envision this being a struggle.

* * *

IN JUST ANOTHER MINUTE, Rose came in and gave Tracy a confused look as she closed the door of the shop behind her.

"What's with the banner outside?"

Tracy had arrived early to hang the *"Temporarily Closed While We Prepare for the Grand Opening of the New In Season"* sign.

"Remember our agreement, Aunt Rose?"

"OK… OK…. but I cannot stay closed too long or we will never recover lost customers."

"Fair enough. You are going to have to change with the times, Aunt Rose. Like it or not. I know you love to talk about the good old days, and how you and Uncle Frank used to do things. But if you want to keep this place open and make it a going enterprise again, we need to try some new approaches."

Rose nodded, but Tracy could see she was not real sure. Tracy motioned to Rose to follow her to the back where she had sketched out a strategy. Rose looked at the designs and notes and Tracy could tell this was going to be a harder sell than she had imagined.

"My idea is to select a popular flower each few months and make that the centerpiece showcase around which everything else revolves. To begin with, I chose the carnation."

"Carnations? Really?" Rose asked. "Pretty common flower in my opinion."

"Perhaps, but popular with the world nonetheless. Did you know, for example, that the carnation dates back over 2000 years? They are rich in symbolism and mythology as well."

Rose did not reply.

"And each color is attached to an emotion: white for love and good luck, while red is seen for admiration and deeper love and affection while purple colors imply vulnerability or fickleness. Most impactful are the pink colors, though. This variety originates from the story that they first appeared from the Virgin Mary's tears which became symbolic for a mother's undying love."

"And that helps us, how?"

"You need to really market your products, Aunt Rose. They are not just flowers. I am telling you, from my experience at CMB, that an elaborate story behind something simple—or common as you put it about the carnation—makes the ordinary seem extraordinary."

"I guess…why did you leave that fancy-schmancy job anyway?"

"Aunt Rose, can you please not bring that up. I am here to help you out until I can figure out what is next for me."

"Sure…sorry. I did not mean to bring that up again."

Tracy then went back to her designs to explain in more detail to Rose just how this was going to work and what other flowers she might consider down the road as different focal points to avoid having one type get stale and predictable.

"Think change and innovation and allure, Aunt Rose…."

Just then there was a sharp knock at the front door. They both looked up suddenly wondering who this could be as the closed sign with the announcement of a relaunch was clearly visible. Tracy went to check and felt her spirits sink as she saw who had come calling. Before opening the door and greeting the visitor, Tracy turned to her aunt.

"Hate to ruin your day, Aunt Rose, but it would appear your competition has arrived. I am guessing the signage was too much of a curiosity factor to ward her off."

Rose looked to the closed door, and like Tracy, had no idea the day could get any worse. Never say never she mumbled to herself…

Carnations and Deadly Fixations
FERN GROVE COZY MYSTERY
ABBY REEDE

9 798847 844840